ELLIS ISLAND

TO THE

LAST BEST WEST

FREDDA J. BURTON

Introduction

This story is the second in a series detailing the life and times, both good and bad, of Klara Larsson. By the early 1900's when Klara reached Ellis Island, nearly a quarter of the population of Sweden had immigrated to America. Some were running away from something—conscription into the army, grinding poverty, dwindling family farms. Others ran towards something—religious freedom, vast farm land, jobs, and happiness, both real and imagined.

Klara was no different. her family lived on the brink of extinction on a small patch of a farm in central Sweden. She gathered up her courage and traveled west to what was billed as the 'Last, best West' at the tender age of sixteen. Our story continues her tale.

The characters and events are fictional. They grew from stories told by my grandparents and friends and from old homesteading accounts. Perkins County, South Dakota is a real place with a rich history. I grew up in Butte County south of Bison in Perkins County and visited the original homestead of my grandparents on occasion. No trace of their sod house or the frame house erected in Coal Springs can be found. Only the stories remain.

The illustrations are mine. The drawings in the beginning of the story are in the style of old Swedish wall paintings. The stiff figures and huge flower plumes are typical. The flower plumes hovering over the figures are called 'kurbits' and represent the gourd vine God sent to protect Jonah from the harsh sun at Nineveh. As Klara becomes more 'Americanized,' the kurbits disappear from the drawings.

The diary entries made by Torval are distilled from an actual diary kept by my grandfather, Charles Hanson, in 1900. The spelling, grammar, and abbreviations are his own.

Thanks to all who read the manuscript, offered stories or pictures, and urged me on to finish the story.

Old Ways, New Days

~~Klara~~

A fluttering piece of waste paper in the road, a bed sheet drying on a line, a child's shirt-tail whipping with the wind reproached Klara, reminded her of the lost apron. Brand new and store-bought, made of the thinnest gauze and meant for Sunday wear, her sister, Stina, had given it to her just before she began her journey to America that bright spring day in 1900. *If only I had held it tighter or not listened to Sophia's demand to take it off.* Klara turned the events of the morning through her mind with the feeble hope she could change the scene and repair the damage. She thought back to the morning, the morning of her first real day in America. How long ago it seemed now.

She remembered the sun slanting in through the upper panes of the tall windows of the Ellis Island infirmary as she awakened with the dust motes. Had she been a fly on the wall she would have seen herself, the dark-haired girl in the third bed, awake, startled and confused.

Arrival at Ellis Island

Though Klara had been in the ward for nearly a week and away from her home in Sweden more than a month, she still expected to hear her father stirring in the bed closet across the room, expected to hear the meadow thrush greeting the dawn outside her window. Then, when she finally remembered she was not at home, she would rise up slowly, expecting to hit her head on the low ceiling of the ship's cabin. It was only when she was sitting up on the side of the high ward bed with its stiff sheets did she realize she was in America. Home was far across the ocean; the long voyage was over, and she was waiting to learn if she would be sent back or allowed entrance into the United States. How awful to faint in the processing line, she thought, then blushed with the memory of coming to her senses with a man undoing her blouse, pressing the cold stethoscope to her bare skin.

But today, today she was to be discharged from the infirmary and allowed to go before the examiners in the Great Hall. The day nurse spoke enough Swedish to convey this to Klara, but not enough to reassure her that this was a formality. Most of the immigrants believed that any sign of illness or weakness would send them back to the old country and Klara had not been informed that her illness was the combination of exhaustion, heat, and a virulent bug circulating among the steerage passengers of the *Charlotta*. Over a hundred had been confined to the ship until the infection ran its course. Only Klara had made it as far as the processing center before she was felled by the fever and chills as she waited her turn. Now she was afraid she might be sent back or, perhaps worse, pass inspection only to find herself alone in this strange country.

Which would be harder, she wondered as she gathered up stockings, pantaloons, slip, and dress under the watching eyes of the ward matron, then followed her down the hall to the shower room. For a girl familiar with an occasional bath in a zinc tub with water heated on the wood stove, the shower with running hot and cold water was a marvel. The pleasure of standing under the pulse of hot water, the smooth lather of soap, the rough towel was heaven. As she washed her long hair, Klara wondered if rich old Mrs. Lof, her neighbor back home, had any thing as fine as this.

After braiding her hair into a tight coil which she pinned into a roll at the nape of her neck, Klara dressed in her one spare outfit, her Sunday black skirt and white blouse. She hesitated, then unrolled the new apron still wrapped in its paper shroud. Stina had wrapped it and put it in Klara's bag just before the sisters had said goodbye. Though reserved for church and holidays, Klara decided this day was special enough to wear the thin gauzy apron. After she tied the white apron over her dark skirt, she shook the wrinkles from her head scarf and put it on. For a brief moment she wished for a sweeping picture hat, perhaps rose-colored with a long plume. Silly child, she scolded herself. She packed the rest of her belongings under the watching eyes of the other inmates of the ward, then walked down the long hallway into a new day.

~~~

How happy she had been to see the familiar face of her old friend, Sophia, in the waiting room of the Ellis Island processing hall. She was even a little bit glad to see Arvid, Sophia's slick-haired husband, though she was still a little frightened of him. She was almost as happy when the last official in the long line of examiners stamped her papers and welcomed her to the United States of America.

After spending a week in the infirmary the world seemed exciting, inviting to Klara. She had been so busy on the voyage across the Atlantic. Her job as nursemaid to the Ersson family had been grueling at best with the seasick Maja, the injured child, Lisa, and two rambunctious boys to watch. She had had no sleep the night before the ship docked, then she was forced to disembark alone and take the ferry to Ellis Island with the steerage passengers. The day was hot and her homespun wool dress had clung to her like a shroud through the long wait in line. The noise and confusion had finally overwhelmed her. When she came to her senses, Klara was in the island infirmary. In the days that followed she saw only her ward-mates with whom she shared no common language, a kind nurse who spoke enough Swedish to calm her worst fears, and a chubby little man in a white coat, a doctor she assumed. When she was well enough, she spent her days walking up and down the halls or gazing out over the fog-bound coast at the tall buildings of New York. Now she was going to see those buildings up close, walk the streets, breathe that heavy air.

Papers in hand Klara rushed across the waiting room. Sophia thrust her ruffled parasol into Arvid's hand, plucked up her long skirt, and ran to meet her. For an instant the two girls embraced, then they jerked apart. Klara put her hand to her cheek and stared at Sophia. Stared at her bright lips and rouged cheeks, her wide-brimmed hat decorated with feathers and fat silk roses. Open-mouthed she gazed at Sophia's tightly cinched waist and high-thrust bosom covered with yards and yards of silk taffeta. Could this fancy lady really be her childhood chum. Then Sophia opened her mouth to speak and revealed the gap-toothed mouth of poverty and Klara knew that fine clothes and rouge could not hide the real Sophia.

~~~

How bright everything seems, thought Klara. She struggled to keep up with Sophia and Arvid on the busy street. She also tried to keep track of the boy with the handcart hired to trundle her box to the train station. If she got separated from them she would be lost forever. So many people pushing past, rushing past, with bundles and baskets, paper-wrapped parcels and armloads of clothing, hay, harness, even a boy toting a dress maker's dummy taller than himself. She almost forgot to keep her eyes on Sophia's aqua blue dress swirling ahead when she heard a bold rooster crow from inside a woven basket tied to the side of a passing cart. It was the sound of home in the midst of this New York racket. Sophia's high, lispy voice brought her back.

"Hurry up, Klara. Don't be gawking at this trash."

Sophia stood primly on the crowded walk with her elbows drawn in, both hands holding the edges of her wide-brimmed hat. Did she think some street child or an errant breeze might snatch it from her.

"Arvid promised ice cream before the train leaves."

"Don't count on it, cupcake."

Arvid grabbed his wife's arm and steered her along the sidewalk. Klara hurried to catch up. She had a hundred questions, but felt it was not the time to ask. Arvid seemed even more abrupt and impatient than she remembered. He had been especially sharp when Sophia stopped on the walkway outside the processing center to complain about Klara's apron. She squeezed her eyes shut and the scene seared across her mind.

"Take it off."

Sophia was fumbling with Klara's apron ties, her small hands crumpling and pleating the thin fabric in her haste.

"Nobody wears them here."

Startled by her friend's out burst, Klara pulled away. "Please don't, Sophia." She tried to smooth the apron over her skirt, protect it from Sophia's nervous fingers. She gave up after nearly dropping her bag and the sheaf of papers from the processing and tried to step away.

Arvid interrupted their bickering. "Sophia's right. Let's get going." He reached for her arm, but Sophia squirmed away. With a shrug he jammed his hands in his pockets and walked towards the ferry landing. "Damn women," he muttered, loud enough for them to hear.

When Klara turned to follow Arvid, Sophia yanked at the thin apron hard enough to tear it. With a giggle she captured the offending apron. Holding it high, she ran to catch up with Arvid. Near tears, Klara followed.

"Let me have it, Sophia. I'll put away. I promise." She remembered how her own sisters had teased Sophia to tears long ago. So this is how it feels, she thought.

Red-faced, Arvid stepped between the two women. "I'll take it," he said. He snatched the apron and wadded it into a small lump. He looked at Klara as if daring her to object and laughed when he saw the memory of another event crawl across her face.

"Give it to me, Arvid." Last summer's going away party flooded her mind, the party her family held to mark the end of Sophia and Arvid's visit to the old country. After a few too many drinks Arvid had taken one of her mother's heirloom cups to raise a toast. When Klara tried to rescue the cup, he had taunted her and slipped outside. Klara followed him into the dark yard where she was forced to trade a kiss for the antique cup. She could still feel his rough mouth, smell the sour home made *brannvin* on his breath. As she reached for her precious apron, she knew his thoughts matched her own. He would never give it to her.

Arvid tossed the wadded apron from hand-to-hand, then pretended to juggle it. The white apron held its balled up shape until he tossed a little too high. A fierce breeze caught it and bellied the white fabric like a sail. It whipped and floated over-head, then blew along dock just out of reach.

"Grab it, please." Klara nearly pitched over the edge of the pier in her attempt to catch the apron. A piece of her old life was ripping away.

Sobered, Sophia begged Arvid. "Do something." She tried to reach it with her frilly parasol, but failed.

Arvid made one vigorous leap for the apron, but the wind whipped it out over the water. A passing barge blocked it from view, but there could be little doubt that the thin bit of cloth would soon be a speck in the scum of trash floating on the harbor. Klara squeezed her eyes shut and turned away to hide her tears.

Jabber and Jello Moulds

"Up and at em, sleepyhead," called Sophia.

At the sound of Sophia's voice Klara opened her eyes expecting to find herself on the pier. Confused by a blast of noise from the street, she rolled out of bed and landed in a tangle of bed clothes on the floor.

"Silly. Here's the baby. He needs changing and a bath."

"Oh. So sorry."

Klara scrambled up and took the drowsy baby on her arm and struggled into her wrapper. Twisting her hair back off her face, she asked Sophia to show her the baby things.

"I think we can move the basinet in here. It'll be more convenient for you."

Klara looked around the tiny room with dismay. How can anything else fit, she wondered. It's smaller than a bed closet. Her lumpy mattress filled the entire space between the door and the small chest under the window.

A cry from the warm bundle in her arms refocused Klara's wandering thoughts. The baby scrunched up his tiny mouth for a louder blast and she could feel his body stiffen against her arm.

"Keep him quiet or the neighbors complain," said Sophia. "That horrid woman. Says her son works nights and needs his sleep."

Left with the baby, Klara began the process of concocting a system to ready herself for the day while keeping the child occupied and content. Wash self, wash baby. No. Wash baby, half wash self. Diaper baby, feed baby. What is this stuff Sophia gives her child. And a bottle with a soft nipple. How smart. She remembered the days she had spent squeezing milk into her baby sister's unwilling mouth from a clean rag. Well this one is willing enough.

With the baby propped on the bed sucking voraciously Klara

dressed and made ready for the day. In the tiny kitchen she surprised Sophia paging through a magazine filled with fashionable ladies.

"Oh. You're a quick one," said Sophia. "Look at these darling camisoles."

"Where do the soiled baby things go?"

"Um. The bucket in the back hall. On the way to the toilet."

~~~

Through that day and most of the next, Sophia instructed Klara in the ways of the household. Soil buckets, wash tubs, cooking pots, flat irons heating on the stove, dirty dishes, dirty floors, dirty children, and Sophia lounging nearby with an illustrated paper or a bit of sewing or embroidery. So much to take in, so much to remember that it made Klara's head buzz. Thankfully, her greatest fear had not materialized. Sophia's lecherous husband, Arvid, was away drumming up business for the shipping company he shilled for.

How small this house will seem with a man around. Flat, she corrected herself, not house. Sophia had spent some time explaining the various living spaces in the city. The squalid tenements with whole families living in walled off sections of hallways with no light and egress only through another family's living room frightened her the most, but tales of nine grownups and uncounted children sharing an eight by twelve room by bunking one a top another and cooking in the doorway seemed impossible. Sophia said it was common enough and that they worked three weeks out of four to pay the rent.

The Big City

"Where did you live when you first arrived?" said Klara.

"This place is a palace, believe me," said Sophia. "Three rooms, water right in the sink, windows and only three flights up."

"Does anyone have a garden?" Klara was thinking about the blank wall that faced the little window in her room. "I feel so confined. Wound about with brick and plaster like a shroud."

"You sound like a German. They're always messing with flowers. Posies in boxes at their windows, green stuff around the saloon doors."

"Sounds nice."

"We'll walk by way of Germantown when we take Lily and Matty out for air."

"Another town? How can we walk so far?"

"Silly. City folks name their neighborhoods like little towns. It's only a few streets over."

"And Arvid calls this Little Boston. How confusing."

"You'll get used to it. Wait until you go to language school. Your head will be spinning like a top."

"It's a wonder we ever found each other."

"Well, that's a fact. Without Arvid we'd both be sleeping in the gutter."

~~~

One bright morning Klara found Sophia busy in the kitchen surrounded with bowls, measuring cups, and spoons. She was squinting at a small pasteboard box with red lettering.

"Put Matty in his highchair and help me with this," she said.

"What a mess."

"Figure this out. I'll get the tin mould."

Klara took the box and held it to the light streaming in the window. The print was small and in English of course. Exasperated, she threw the box on the table and went to move a howling kettle from the stove.

"Your water's boiling. Are you having tea?" She glanced over to see Sophia balanced on a chair reaching for the fluted mould on the shelf over the door.

"Dump the stuff in the box into that bowl, then measure out a cup of the hot water."

"What?"

"I think that's what it says on the box."

When Klara poured the steaming water onto the powder, a strong aroma filled the kitchen. Klara nearly dropped the cup.

"Stir it, Klara. Quick, or it will be all lumps."

"Oh. It's red. And smells like strawberries."

"Jello, they call it. Here, let me stir. Get cold water next."

"And wash the tin?"

That night the boiled potatoes and steamed carrots were forgotten in the rush to unmold the Jello for a first taste. The two girls took turns spooning up the jiggly dessert for the children and tasting it for themselves.

"More," begged Lily.

"Oh. We've eaten it all."

"So good," said Sophia. "I'll get more at the grocery tomorrow."

"What should I do with the potatoes?"

"Next time we eat them first. Icebox. They'll keep."

On The Move

A week or so later, Arvid, red-faced and sweaty, plopped himself down at the supper table and spread an armload of papers amidst the plates and cutlery.

"Did you sign up lots of travelers?" said Sophia. "The rent is due tomorrow."

"Railroads. That's where the action is."

"The rent. I need the rent money."

"No one is going back to the old country these days."

Klara sat back and studied Arvid more carefully. Did he seem nervous. More frantic than excited.

"Lily needs a new dress. And I saw a darling hat yesterday."

Arvid seemed to see his wife for the first time. He pushed a few pamphlets across the table in her direction.

"Look at these. Just look. We could have a house. And a garden. Fresh air."

"But we'd have to move again."

"Umm. Progress. Railroad is thinking to build spur lines in the Midwest. Dakota, Iowa, northern Minnesota, maybe into Wyoming. If we could get in on the ground floor, we could rake in the bucks."

"Bucks?" said Klara.

"Dollars, greenbacks, Jack, simoleons, cash."

Thinking about the sweaty, hard-muscled men she had seen laying rail back in Sweden, she said, "Isn't it terribly hard work?"

Arvid stared at her for a moment before a grin creased his face. "Not pick and shovel stuff. I'd be in on the planning, buying and selling and stuff."

"What about free land?"

"Not much of that left. Heard a rumor though. Government may open up some reservation land in a few years."

"Government reserve land?" said Sophia.

"No. Indian treaty land. In the Dakotas. Our Klara, here, could become a homesteader."

"Me? Why not you and Sophia?"

"Ha. Work, work, and more work. We'd have calluses up to our elbows."

"Well. None of this chit-chat is getting the rent paid." Sophia motioned to Klara. "I think the baby is awake."

"Sorry. I'll check."

While she changed the baby and soothed Lily back to sleep, she listened to the voices penetrating the thin walls.

"Now. We need to go now. Before we pay another dime to that pinchfist."

"Can't we wait?"

"The season for returning to old Svenska is about over for this year."

"What about Klara?"

"She'll have to pay her own way."

Klara spent sleepless hours wondering how much the fare would be. Would her small stash of money cover it. To stay in the city alone was beyond her imagining. She had to stick with Sophia. Near dawn she fell asleep, only to be shaken awake soon after.

"Get up, Klara. You need to help."

"What? Oh, Sophie, let me sleep."

"We got to pack. Now."

Klara had not yet unpacked her own trunk, so she managed to dress and pile her night clothes and few personal things into her bag before Sophia pushed her into the kitchen.

"The boy can load your stuff on the cart while you pack up the utensils and dishes. I'll get the baby things."

Klara began placing items into the waiting crate.

"Hurry. Don't bother with those big pots. Put the food in the wicker basket, then come help me with Lily."

Plates and cups wrapped roughly in a linen table cloth went into the box along with cast iron frying pans, enamel coffee pot and grinder. Klara tried to remember the items used most often. What about Sophia's pretties arranged on the shelf above the door. Arvid settled that question when he burst in with the baby held out in front of him.

"Change this varmint, then get him dressed."

"My trunk?"

"Already on the cart. Here's your bag. Keep track of it."

While Klara tended to Matty, she caught glimpses of Arvid maneuvering beds and dressers through the narrow doorways to the stair head where a pair of stout young fellows took over. By the time the children were ready the men were arguing over a carved highboy.

"Won't fit, man."

"Of course it will. It came up. It has to go down."

"My aching back. You can't pay me enough."

"Sophie, Klara, get the brats down to the street so we can finish up here."

"But I'm not done," wailed Sophia. "I need more boxes."

"Better we leave some of the house plunder, than end up in the pokey."

In the kitchen Klara added paper packets of coffee, sugar, a loaf of bread and a wedge of cheese waiting for next morning's breakfast to her bag. With Arvid's strident commands pulling her to the door and the baby heavy on her shoulder she looked up at the shelf above the door. Sophia's pretties peered back at her: copper molds, figurines of dogs and children, gilded teacups. So sad to leave them, she thought. Sophia will be heartbroken. She reached for a graceful lady with a sleek wolfhound at her side and placed it carefully in her bag. There, she thought. Sophia will have one of her nice things.

"Now," said Arvid. "Get going. Now. No arguing."

He pushed Sophia and Lily out the door and Klara followed. In the street they found the young men struggling to wedge the highboy onto an already overloaded cart.

"Leave it, man," said Arvid. "I'll flag a cabbie for the women and come with you."

Klara followed Sophia and Arvid to the cab stand at the corner. Though it was late, the street and sidewalks teemed with people hurrying every which way. Does this place ever sleep, she wondered.

14

Moving Day

At the train station the noise, confusion, and bright light hit them like a wave. Klara would have clapped her hands over her ears if she hadn't been clutching her bag and the baby so tightly. She stood close to Sophia, while they waited for Arvid to arrange for shipment of their household goods.

"Where are we going?"

"Duluth or Sioux Falls, maybe. Arvid has mentioned several places."

"Is it very far?"

"I wish we could settle someplace and never move again."

"You've done this before?"

"Two months rent owing. Butcher's bill unpaid. Arvid figures we make a good profit moving."

There was no answer for this, so Klara turned her attention to the restless baby.

~~~

The train jerked away from the station, made a few more quick stops to load freight and passengers, then settled into a smooth, rumbling klickity-klack across the hours. At full light Klara parceled out the bread and cheese which they washed down with tea purchased from the porter.

"Five cents for tea," stormed Arvid. "Robbers."

"How far are we going?" said Sophia. "Your collar is all crooked, Arvid."

She, herself, looked a bit disheveled, but still stylish in a high-collared, pleated shirtwaist and long skirt with its sheaf of lace petticoat showing. Her hat with its plumes and beads sat on the rack above balanced on someone's satchel.

Seated next to her friend, Klara seemed like a gray mouse in her plain homespun dress, woolen cloak, and heavy boots. She watched the other travelers pulling out food from bags and baskets. Most had prepared ahead of time or bought box lunches at the station. She looked at Arvid seated across from her.

"If tea is so much, how will we eat when the bread is gone?"

"We should've got box lunches at the station," said Sophia. "So much cheaper."

"Not to worry. We make a stop around ten."

But at ten, the train was still moving through open country at top speed and Arvid was forced to cough up more of his precious coin to purchase sandwiches and lemonade. Despite her guilty conscience, Klara enjoyed her fare immensely.

By evening the restless children and cramped space drove Arvid to the club car. Left to themselves Sophia and Klara settled Lily and the baby on Arvid's vacant seat and amused themselves by making up stories about the world scrolling by their window. When full dark descended, Sophia found another amusement.

"Can you manage here for a bit?" she asked Klara. "I'll be right back."

She returned ten minutes later with a deck of cards, a note pad and pencil, and several bananas.

"Might as well have a bit of fun," said Sophia.

"Make the best of it, huh?" said Klara. She accepted a banana and helped Sophia clear a level space for the cards. "*Patience?* We played it at the Loft's sometimes."

"Do you know *Demons and Thieves?*"

"No. Just *Clock*. And *Pyramid*."

The girls shuffled their way through several hours, taking turns laying out the cards in rows and circles, playing red on red or alternating colors to complete sets and sequences. *Demons* with its double columns proved to be too great a challenge for their tired minds, so they plowed through endless games of the simpler variety. It was past midnight when Sophia pushed the cards away.

"Have you ever traveled so far?" said Klara. "We must be clear across the country by now."

"Chicago, maybe. Wake me up when we get there."

"Twenty-four hours. Who knew a train could go so long."

She picked up the cards and stuffed them in her satchel, then helped Sophia get more comfortable. The cold glass of the window seemed a comfy pillow when she finally relaxed against it.

Near dawn the train slowed and began a shrill whistling to signal many crossings. After an endless crawl through dingy neighborhoods it stopped with a bump and a lurch. Half asleep, Klara grabbed up her bag and one of the sleeping children and followed Sophia down the narrow aisle to the steep iron step of the rail car where Arvid reached up to take her burdens. Almost before they knew it they were huddled on the platform.

"Where are we?" demanded Sophia.

"It looks just like New York," said Klara.

"All train stations look alike," said Arvid. "This is Chicago."

With a wail Sophia said she didn't want to live in another dirty city and the babies joined her lament with their howls.

"Hush up. We're not staying, just changing trains," said Arvid.

"Another train? You mean we're not there yet?" Sophia looked as if she would burst into tears. "I'm sooo tired."

Klara with the baby in her arms sat down on a nearby bench and beckoned Sophia to bring the older child to her.

"Here. Rest a bit."

"I'll check the schedule and find our track," said Arvid. He disappeared into the crowd, leaving the two women to worry alone.

~~~

Klara pointed to the seemingly endless rows of posters tacked to various surfaces on the platform. A few bits of red, white, and blue bunting trailed from some of them. "Who are these fellows?"

"Umm. Politics. There's an election in the fall."

"That one with the mustaches. He must be important."

"Teddy Roosevelt. He wants to be vice president."

"Of Chicago?"

"No silly. Of the whole country. He must have campaigned here for there to be so many pictures. The candidates come through on special train cars and speechify to the crowds."

"And then what happens?"

"In November everybody votes and the winner gets the job."

"He becomes the king?"

"No, no, no. The president. And Roosevelt will only be the helper to the president. If his party wins, that is. And only till the next election."

"Sounds like a lot of bother," said Klara.

"Arvid better hurry up. These kiddels are about to start howling."

"Speak of the devil," muttered Klara.

"What?"

"Here comes Arvid."

Both women jumped up and plied Arvid with questions which he seemed not to hear. He gestured towards a sign board and hurried off without a word. Klara and Sophia struggled to keep him in sight as they juggled children and bags, dodged passengers and baggage carts, then reached the relative quiet of a smaller section of the station.

With barely a pause they followed him down a long passageway to a different area of the rail yard. Here the platforms were smaller with signs of construction still in evidence. A yard engine maneuvered cars to form up a new configuration of passenger cars, baggage cars, and freight. Porters and messenger boys scurried in every direction.

Arvid stopped short and told them wait, don't budge from this spot.

"What's going on, Arvid?" said Sophia.

"We need to change trains is all."

"What about our stuff?"

"Don't worry, love. They move the baggage car to the other train. This train. That's what the little engine is for."

"Where are we going?"

"If you'd bother to read the signs, you'd know."

He pointed to a board above the platform. A boy balanced on a ladder scrambled to add numbers to the list of cities which included Minneapolis, Sioux City, Sioux Falls, and Grand Forks.

Sophia complained, "It's a just a jumble. Which town is ours?"

"Towns? Where?" said Klara. She peered where Sophia pointed. Though she squinted her eyes, she could make out nothing but squiggles on the train board.

"It's in English, silly," said Sophia. She continued to bicker with Arvid until their train pulled into the station.

The train west was shabby and consisted of two passenger cars in a long line of freight cars carrying materials to extend the rail line past its present stopping point. Though Arvid had insisted the baggage car would be transferred to their new train, they found their baggage heaped at the end of the row of seats. The house plunder was stashed in the corner of a lumber car according to the porter Arvid accosted. Arvid dismissed this development with a shrug of his shoulders, but became visibly agitated when he discovered the train had no dining or club car. While Sophia and Klara settled the children, he went in search of the car attendant.

The train had clacked and huffed its way past the city limits before they heard Arvid's strident voice complaining to all who would listen. By the time he slumped into the seat next to Sophia he had damned the entire staff of the railroad from the president on down to the bent old black man who swept out the carriages.

"Hush, Arvid. Everyone is staring," said Sophia. "We'll be okay."

"It's the principle. How can they treat me so."

"The porter said the train stops for water in about an hour. We can get something to eat then."

By the time the train disgorged the weary group onto the platform at Sioux Falls, Klara no longer cared about schedules and final destinations or even food. Exhausted, she sat on her trunk and vowed to never set foot on another train. She turned a deaf ear to Sophia's pleas and demands to look after the children. Nothing, it seemed, would rouse her to action.

Ignoring the women and crying children, Arvid set about checking schedules and alternate transportation. He seemed to have some definite goal in mind as he paged through notices and questioned station personnel. When he returned to Sophia and Klara, he was brimming with news and ideas.

"We can head west in the morning. A work train is scheduled

for Montana and they have room for our stuff."

"Montana?" said Sophia. "Why Montana. What's there?"

"I hired on to boss a work crew. They'll advance us enough for a week."

"Why hire you. They don't even know who you are."

"I can read and write. That's more than you can say for the work crew."

"Where will we stay?"

"You'll need a ticket. Klara, too."

"More money?"

"I found a place to stay tonight. Cheap."

Arvid had made arrangements for a room in a flophouse near the station and now herded Sophia and the children out of the station and down the street. Klara brought up the rear dragging her trunk.

By the time Klara realized she was to share the narrow room with Arvid and Sophia, she had already opened her small stash and handed over a precious dollar bill. Arvid laughed and called her a tightwad.

Sophia giggled. "Don't worry, Klara. He'll find a card game and not show his face here till morning."

Weary from the long journey, Klara fell into a deep sleep the minute she laid down. When she awoke, she was alone in the room. With growing dismay she felt for her money pouch at her waist. It was gone. Struggling to clear the fog from her brain, she saw the embroidered bag on the dresser. Only then did she realize her money was gone along with Sophia, the children, and their baggage. Sophia, or perhaps even Arvid, had slipped the purse away while she slept.

How could they. Klara couldn't decide between anger and panic. What to do. She wanted to rage through the streets and scream the guilty pair back to face justice. An instant later fear grabbed at her throat and she collapsed on the bed.

A tiny knock at the door roused her. Had they had a change of heart. But, no. It was a boy's voice calling through the thin door.

"Your hot water, miss. I'll be leaving it here," called the youngster who worked as a porter at the hotel.

Klara opened the door and helped the boy place the pitcher of hot water on the wash stand. She questioned him and was gratified when he answered in Norwegian, a language close enough to her own that she had no trouble understanding.

"You work here?"

"Pay isn't much, but they give room and board."

"Did you see the man who paid for this room?"

"Said you'd be down later. He was with the fancy lady and her kiddos. Seemed to be in a terrible hurry to catch an early train."

"Do you think I could get a job here?"

"Dunno, Miss. Guess I could ask."

By the time Klara had washed up and pinned her long braid into a cornet, a number of people from the hotel and the neighboring cafe had stopped by to check on 'that girl stranded by her dastardly friends.' If this were a Victorian novel, Klara would have been cast into the street, penniless and hungry, to face a bleak future. But, no, this was Sioux Falls, South Dakota, small town America epitomized, and a dozen strangers stepped forward with offers of aid and succor.

"Old Missus Ulner could use a bit of help."

"She has a spare room."

"And she speaks your lingo."

"Mr. Rand here runs the paper. Expect he can help you find something more permanent."

"With pay, he means," said Mr. Rand. "Gotta have the simoleons to make it in this world."

By evening Klara was ensconced in the spare room of the elderly lady. Her trunk had been moved with the general store's handcart, her hand baggage carried by the hotel porter.

"Now then, Miss," said Mr. Rand. "We'll be in touch. Expect we'll find you something suitable quick as a wink."

Diary of Torval Hansen

Turn of the Century Wolf Hunt

The new century, he mused. What will it bring? The tall eighteen-year old stood on the small rise overlooking the road to town. His family's farm spread out behind him, golden in the rising sun. He barely noticed the smooth, clear fields awaiting spring planting or the tight barns shielding fat cattle from the chill morning air. His thoughts focused on the gala dinner he would attend at the Thomas Halverson home that evening. Should he wear the new tie and collar, or would that be too much. Maybe his old dinner jacket would be better. How many pretty gals would Martin scare up for the party.

If it seemed odd to be partying on a Sunday, Torval gave it no thought. Grand Valley School where he was a senior was not in session that week because of the New Year's holiday. Turn of the century fever gripped the small community. A few staunch believers camped out on a nearby hill to await the second coming, some stocked up on coal oil and candles for fear of some sort of governmental collapse, others ignored the milestone completely. Torval and his friends found it the perfect excuse for a dinner party.

January 1, 1900 Monday. The first day of the new century starts up rather cold but no storms. The world is still intact. Dinner at T. Halverson's place was very pleasant.

~~~

Torval stumbled into the kitchen. "Where is everyone?"

"Well, sleepy Joe. When did you drag in last night?" said Hans. "You look like a gnawed dog bone."

"Don't be such a clinchpoop."

"What nonsense are you spewing now, Joe?"

"Just think, it's 1900," said Torval. "And don't call me Joe."

"Sleepy, sleepy Joe. Carrie left you toast and oatmeal in the warming oven."

"Where's Mama?"

"Father said for you to haul corn to Wallquists for grinding. Mother's down with a sick headache."

"Bother it all. I'm on vacation."

"No rest for the wicked. See you at dinner. And watch that mouth."

Torval yelled at his retreating brother. "A clinchpoop is a boor, you dummkopf."

~~~

Torval struggled through the day half asleep. He cheered himself by thinking about the trip he had planned with Martin the night before. The only problem would be the certain outburst of disproval he would suffer from his father and brother. Work, he thought, it's all they're about. He vowed to keep himself out of that rut.

They caught up with him in the dark barn next morning while he saddled a horse. Hans held up his lantern.

"Ha. Lazy Bones can get up early."

"Mighty fine duds for chores. The hogs will appreciate it."

Torval ignored them and led the horse into the yard.

"Going to Meckling with Martin. I'll be home in a couple of days," he said.

January 2, 1900 Tuesday. The second day of the new year is very nice. Martin Halverson & I were in Meckling South Dakota. In the evening we were at H. Mryons, good time. The guests were Mary J., Mary H., Chas. M., Martin & myself.

January 3, 1900 Wednesday. Visited at Knute & Gilbert's. Martin was also at Gayville, S.D. Party in the evening, 10 individuals present. Went home one o'clock.

~~~

"Well, well. The traveler hath returned. Can we expect any work from his highness today?"

Torval's father interrupted, "See that you have the gray horse spiffed up by noon. I think I have a buyer."

Torval hated horses, all horses. He hated their smell. He hated touching their sweaty, twitching hides and course manes. He hated the clank of the metal bit on their huge teeth when he bridled them and the acrid stench that arose when he scraped the rocks from their heavy feet. Sweet little foals and hard muscled broncos, his mother's steady carriage horse or the trio of bay geldings used for everyday work around the farm all gave him a feeling of unease.

Were they waiting to whirl and kick or use those long yellow teeth on his arm or backside. When astride one of the beasts, it seemed to watch him and plot the next hole to stumble over or the next dark shape to shy from. This was a dreadful fix for a boy in rural South Dakota in 1900.

January 4, 1900 Thursday. Favorable weather. In the forenoon Martin & I visited at Ben Larson's. Father sold gray horse. The consideration is $100.00.

~~~

"Torval. Will you favor us with a little work today," said Mr. Hanson, "Or is it more gadding about?"

"He did do a good job on the gray horse," defended Hans. "Clipped him slick as snot. Never know he was wooly as a bear an hour before."

January 5, 1900 Friday. Spring is showing its appearance, but The Missouri River was walked upon by myself. Frozen solid. I visited at H. Petersons in the afternoon.

January 6, 1900 Saturday. Visited N. Larson's, visited at L. Caberly. In the evening I attended a surprise party at Halvorsons.

~~~

And so the first week of 1900 passed in a fury of social events and hard work. It was partly inspired by the turn of the century, partly by the unusually fine January weather. Fear of howling Dakota blizzards and subfreezing temperatures that normally attended the winter months sent all of Lincoln County into a frenzy of visiting, buying, selling, laying in food for man and beast, airing bedding, and mucking out barns.

Though the homesteads of Lincoln and Clay counties were well established by this time, the work was hard and the rewards few and far between. The winter months provided a measure of progress and prosperity, or lack thereof, that often resulted in several defections from the small community.

January 7, 1900 Sunday. Attended services at the Timber Church. Invited to dinner at H. Petersons. In the evening we visited Will Cowman who is giving it up. Farewell.

January 8, 1900 Monday. On this day I took the train for Canton reached this place at 12.05 o'clock, foggy weather. Anton T. received inheritance of $1000. Will he stay on?

January 9, 1900 Tuesday. The atmosphere is cool and cloudy. Theodore Torberson visited here in the evening. Talked of heading to Calif. Wrote letters. Heard that Ingham has sold out and is heading back east.

~~~

"Looks like a change in the weather," announced Hans. "How are you this morning, Mother?"

He kissed the thin, pale women seated at the breakfast table.

Carrie interrupted, "She's much better this morning, aren't you, Momma?'

"Yes, dear. I'm fine. Can you go to town for quilt batting? For the Ladies Aid meeting?"

"See that you get back before the storm hits," said Mr. Hanson.

"Maybe we should wait," said Carrie. She picked at a button on her dress front.

Prairie storms could brew up quickly and with little warning. Carrie, in particular, had reason to be leery. One threatening night when she was in the seventh grade, Carrie and Hans had attended a party some three miles from home. A blizzard raged out of the northwest and stranded them there for several days. When her father and uncle finally came for them, it was on foot. By the time the party struggled home, Carrie's overshoes were frozen to her shoes. She sat by the kitchen stove with her feet propped on the oven door and when they began to thaw, her feet prickled, burned and then hurt. Now, even a little chill sent her running indoors and she wore wool stockings summer and winter.

"Torval. We need more feed ground. Take Carrie. She can shop while you're tending to business," said Mr. Hanson. "See that you're ready for school tomorrow, too."

January 10, 1900 Wednesday. A snow storm is threatening its appearance on this date. No snow yet. Ground feed at J. Wallquists. Papa's harping at me about school.

January 11, 1900 Thursday. Half day at school. Out early for fear of blizzard. No snow. Attended K. P. dance at Bedford Hall. Quite showy.

January 12, 1900 Friday. Storm moved through north of us. Arty Thompson visited here. Took in the Literary Society meeting at the Grand Valley schoolhouse. Good program, good attendance.

January 13, 1900 Saturday. I went to Canton in the afternoon. Large crowd in Canton today. Talk of the wolf hunt everywhere. Attended Crohonals party at L. Flory.

January 14, 1900 Sunday. I attended Sunday school. Arndt Hanson visited here, also Torbersons. Hans and Carrie visited at Billers.

January 15, 1900 Monday. School a bore. Tom Renli visits here today. To-morrow we expect to have a great time hunting wolves. Cloudy looks like snow.

~~~

Carrie shoved the plate of toast across the table to her brother. "You're not dressed for school?"

"Maybe he's studying the fine art of hunting," said his father. "See the tall boots. Does he have his gloves and rifle stashed by the back door?"

"The wolf hunt? You're nixing school to hunt wolves?"

"Tom wanted to go. He's only here for a day or two."

"Tom? Blame it on Tom. How do you expect to graduate?"

"I'm doing okay."

Wolves, once a real menace to the homesteader, were mostly the stuff of legend in Lincoln County. They were blamed for unexplained livestock deaths and disappearances and stories of rare sightings made the day at the barber shop.

"Has anyone even seen one this year?" said Carrie.

"Sam Watson said his brother had one cornered in his sheep shed, but it got clean away."

"Where's this?"

"Over near Herrick."

"Reservation land almost. Miles and miles from here."

~~~

In the pitch black of early morning Torval left the house to walk the half mile to his meeting point with Tom. As he limbered up, he shook off his guilty thoughts of school and parental disapproval. By the time he spied Tom waiting on the high seat of the two wheel gig he was whistling softly to himself. With a quick spring he seated himself beside Tom and stowed his weapon under the seat.

"All set?" said Tom.

"Let's go get the varmints."

Tom clucked to the horse and drove down the farm lane to join the straggly parade of wagons and bicycles moving along the county road. A few horsemen galloped up and down the line of hunters encouraging haste and providing a gala air to the proceedings.

At the staging place the hunt organizers delegated groups of younger boys to fan out to act as beaters with the hope that they would meet up with the beaters working their way towards the bluffs from the west. Tom and Torval held back for fear that they would be asked to join in as they had in previous years. This year they were determined to be among the group to kill or capture any prey driven their way.

"Gore! Can you believe the crowd?" said Tom.

"Must be hundreds out here," said Torval. "And that's not counting the bunch from Meckling."

"Look at that." Tom pointed to a couple of wagoneers who had set out signs advertising ammunition, shooting belts, and box lunches for sale.

"No self respecting wolf is gonna come near here."

"We could head out to the river bluffs."

"By ourselves?"

"Arnst said he heard there was a den below Gage Point."

"Suits me."

They soon left the babble of voices behind. Only the sound of an occasional shot carried across the flat prairie to remind the boys of the grand affair behind them. When they reached the main road, Tom whipped up the horse and they clattered along at a steady trot for a half hour or so. When the river came into view, Tom let the horse slow down to pick his way down the steep track to a wooded area.

"This is more like it," said Tom.

The boys tethered the horse and walked to the edge of the bluff. A faint rustle of the grass told them they were not alone.

"By gore," muttered Torval. "Something's down there."

"Quiet."

"I'll go to the left and down that little cleft. You go right. Maybe you can get a shot if he runs."

Torval inched through the dry brush holding his breath each time a pebble rolled or a sage branch slapped his boot. By the time he reached the cleft in the bluff sweat prickled between his shoulder blades. Movement and a flash of tan froze him

A large jackrabbit outran Tom's rifle sight and disappeared.

January 16, 1900 Tuesday. This was the day of the great wolf hunt. No wolfs captured. Only one jackrabbit. Over 500 people present.

~~~

"No wolfs. Well, well," said Hans. "All that effort and you blew off school to boot."

"See that you attend today," said Carrie. "We need you out of the house for the Aid Society meeting."

"The pelts are worth a dollar this time of year. And they pay 25 cents bounty, too. I could save enough for a bicycle in no time."

"And if I catch this bird and the one roosting in the bush, I'll have two."

"Really. If I had a wheel, I could make it to town in half an hour. Run all your errands. Messages too."

"Dreamer," said Carrie. "Next thing he'll want is one of them auto things people are talking about."

The Curved Dash Oldsmobile was two years from production and would cost the earth because of low production and limited distribution. Henry Ford would form his Ford Motor Company in 1903, but his assembly line would not be up and running until 1913, so it would be years before the 'ninety-three minute' Model T would hit the roads of Lincoln County. Still, rumors of the horseless carriage circulated among the dreamers of the Great Plains States.

January 17, 1900 Wednesday. The Ladies Aid Society of Grand Valley held its semi Monthly meeting here. Good attendance. Mr. & Mrs. Rev. Tetlie also present.

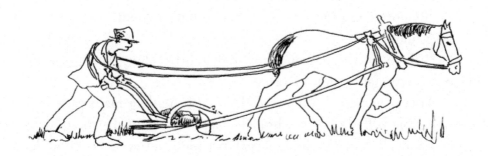

The Wheel

The Hanson farm sat at the cross roads of two carefully laid out roads that divided the township into neat squares outside Canton. The nearest railway passed through Canton on its way to Mitchell, Chamberlain, and points west, but was of little help when it came to the trek to school, rounding up cattle, or planning an excursion to the Buttes or the Missouri River. What was a young man to do.

Torval thought he had the perfect solution in the bicycle. If he only had a little money or help from his parents. Like so many residents of the American Midwest, Torval and his siblings looked forward to the new Sears and Roebuck catalog. Its coming promised a look at the latest fashions, tools, furniture, gizmos and gadgets all promising a better, richer, easier life. It also had six pages extolling the most marvelous bicycles ever.

"Has it come yet?" said Torval.

Just back from town, his brother, Hans, unloaded parcels from the utility wagon and carried them into the kitchen.

"Stop gawking and help," said Hans.

Together, they lifted the fifty pound sack of flour from the wagon bed and lugged it into the pantry. Rice, sugar, and potatoes followed.

When the house stuff was safely stowed, Hans untied the team and flipped the reins to Torval.

"Your turn. Brush them down and see that you give them a full measure of corn."

"Did you bring the mail?"

"See that you hang the harness right, too. It was all in a tangle this morning."

It was noon before Torval made it back to the house where he found Hans pouring over the new catalog.

"Do you see them? The new bikes?" said Torval.

"Look at this hay loader. Boy, would that ever save my back."

"I need to find a way to get some money."

"A job, a job with real wages? Or do you plan to take up bank robbery?"

"I'm not like you. Farming's in your blood. You and Papa," said Torval.

"Now you sound like our brother, Emil. Business school in Sioux Falls. What a waste of money."

Monday morning dawned warm and clear. 56 degrees in January thought Torval, good money making weather. After breakfast he hiked down the road to the Gilbertson place and offered his services. He was put to work loading and hauling hay from the storage barn to the main holding pen. After ten hours of sweaty, itchy work, Torval walked home a dollar richer.

January 22, 1900 Monday. The temperature is quite warm at 56 degrees. Hauled five loads of millet hay on the Gilbertson farm. My wheels are $1.00 closer.

The next morning a northwestern gale pounded down on Lincoln County like a jackhammer. Damnation, thought Torval. There'll be no money today. At breakfast his unhappiness was compounded by the news that the party at the Torkelsons was postponed because of the foul weather.

~~~

On the last day of January the weather cleared. The entire family gathered at breakfast. Carrie helped her mother dish up scrambled eggs, toast, and ham, while the boys pulled up to the table.

"We need to move the cattle out of the barn lot today. To the east pasture I think," said Mr. Hanson. "Any volunteers?"

"The bull, too?" said Hans.

"Yes. He's been cooped up in the barn too long."

"I've got school," said Torval.

"Not today."

"Just remember, the Ladies Aid is meeting here today," said Mrs. Hanson. "Keep your mess outside."

When they approached the barn, they could hear the bull whacking at the side of his pen with his stubby horns. They had rasped the sharp ends of his horns blunt when they brought the animal in from summer pasture, but he still managed to damage the thick timbers of his enclosure.

"We should send him to the sale." said Hans. "He's way too mean."

"It's the dairy in him," said Mr. Hanson. "Gets good calves though."

"Are we just going to open the door and let him out?" said Torval.

The plan was more elaborate than Torval's assessment and the three men spent an hour or two constructing a temporary chute to guide the bull through the barn lot to the first pasture where a half-dozen yearlings nosed around hunting a little dry grass. From there it was hoped they could herd them across the stubble fields to the willow breaks where the rest of the cattle sheltered from the winter.

"Finished with that panel, Torval?"

"I guess. Seems a bit wobbly."

He hammered one last nail through the temporary panel and went to help Hans saddle the horses. The two shaggy animals that normally pulled the buggy or the utility wagon were tethered next to Hans's saddle horse.

"Torval. Take my horse. Father and I will try to encourage the bull from behind while you ride into the pen and show him the way."

"Oh yeah. Let the kid bait the bull," said Torval. "I'll take old Whitey."

"It's your funeral," said Hans. "Papa, let me give you a leg up."

"Maybe he'll walk down the chute by himself," said Torval.

He leaned over the partition and waved his hat. The bull snorted at him and hooked a horn into the wall, but refused to leave the stall.

Resigned, Torval rode into the temporary chute. The bull
shook his head and charged. Torval reined the horse around and
trotted towards the pasture, the bull in pursuit. Hans and Mr. Hanson
rode behind to keep the bull moving in the right direction.

All went according to plan until Torval, spooked by the bull's
heavy breathing behind him, yanked his horse through a gap in the
fencing and fell off over the animal's head to land in the weeds by the
chicken house. The bull snorted and pawed the ground, then
followed. His horns hooked right and left and sent the panels flying.
Torval watched, helpless, as his brother charged through the gap to
corner the bull in the narrow barn lot. When Hans tried to turn the
bull back towards the pasture, he collided with his father's horse.
Bull, horse, and Mr. Hanson went down. The bull leaped up first,
shook himself mightily, then trotted back through the gap.

Hans let out a whoop and ran the bull into the pasture. After securing the gate, he returned to the barn lot where he found Torval kneeling beside his father.

"Papa's hurt," said Torval. "Get help."

"Blood. The horn musta caught him."

"Can we get him to the house?"

"You dummy. It's all your fault."

The ladies of the Aid Society shrieked and clucked when the boys carried their groaning burden through the front door, but quickly became an efficient squad of helpers. Mr. Hanson was placed on the parlor sofa, while Hans went looking for the doctor.

After a visit from Dr. Sorenson, it was decided that the patient had a cracked rib and a few contusions. A week in bed was the recommendation.

January 31, 1900 Wednesday. Aid Society met with Mrs. Sam Johnson. Mad bull attacks father, severe injuries.

~~~

February continued mild, but the strain between the two brothers continued to fester. Though Mr. Hanson was well on his way to recovery, Hans still blamed Torval for the wreck and the extra work that ensued. Everyone in the family busied themselves with their own projects and spoke seldom.

After morning chores Carrie walked the mile to her cousin's farm to work at stitching a quilt for the Ladies Aid. Hans made several trips to Canton, then found an excuse to take the train into Sioux Falls to stay with a cousin for a few days. Numerous peddlers visited the farm during the week. Encouraged by the mild weather, they were scurrying throughout the county selling all manner of remedies, ribbons, and household helpers. Torval considered investing his few dollars on the area's first lottery until his mother found out and forbid it as gambling.

As February marched on, the Literary Society met, a dance was held in Anton Thomson's large barn, and Torval decided to take a part in the spring play, "Hans Von Smash." He and Carrie spent many evening practicing their dialogue for the production. Torval had the part of Henry Dasher.

"Well done, Carrie," said Torval. "We'll have them cracking up in the aisles."

"Thank you, brother. You're not half bad yourself."

"How do you think papa is doing?"

"Complained about the 'damn pap' we were feeding him. Expect he'll be up for supper in a day or so."

"Hans is going to butcher the bull. Guess he better get on with it."

"Papa wonders why you haven't been spending any time with him."

"Busy. And besides, it was all my fault."

"Nonsense. Surely he doesn't blame you?"

"Hans does."

~~~

With the help of several neighbors and a visitor the butchering went off without a hitch. Since they were already in the business, they butchered a fattened hog at the same time. The helpers were sent home with generous portions of the beef. It was mainly suitable for boiling and grinding because of the age of the animal.

Torval found himself assigned to cleaning and salting the hide. When he finally had the huge, slippery mass laid out to dry in the sun, the Syvertsons and the Wallquists were loading their wagon to return home.

"That was some big critter wasn't it, boy?" said Mr. Wallquist.

"Yes, Sir," said Torval. "Fat too."

"Make a lot of shoes with that hide."

"Guess we'll be hauling it to town to sell."

February 19, 1900 Monday. Mr. & Mrs. Renli visits here. Butchered Bull and hog. Andrew Syvertson assists us. J. Wallquist took ¼ share of Bull.

February 20, 1900 Tuesday. Took Bull's hide to town to-day and also listened to court. Hide weighed 74 lbs 4 ½ oz.

~~~

February finished up cold and disagreeable with few opportunities for Torval to add to his bicycle fund. Freedom of the open road and the wind in his face seemed far away. Hans hauled a load of oats to town near the end of the month where the grain fetched 17 cents a bushel, but the chance for actual wages did not materialize until mid March.

"Torberson stopped by last night. Needs help shelling corn," said Mr. Hanson.

"He sure has a barn full of the stuff," said Hans. "Too bad I have to go to town today."

"Torval?"

"I'm on my way."

March 17, 1900 Saturday. Torberson, assisted by Doc Renli and myself, shelled out 414 bushels of corn.

March 19, 1900 Monday. Shelling corn. Renli being the only co-laborer. Wheel fund grows by $4.00.

"Well, I'm off to the corn mines," said Torval. He pushed away from the breakfast table and prepared to bolt out the door.

"Not today. The home front needs you." said Hans. "We have corn too, you know."

"He's right," said Mr. Hanson. "Too much gadding around the countryside for you, boy."

"I'll never get my wheels," groaned Torval. He threw down his cap and slouched back to his chair.

"Watch it, son. You're not too old for a whipping."

March 23, 1900 Friday. Hanson Bros. Marketed 5 loads corn to-day. Price 22 cts bushel.

March 24, 1900 Saturday Cold and blustery. Hans hauled a load corn to-day.

March 25, 1900 Sunday. Windy. Sunday school at Grand Valley School House.

~~~

"Theo Holter is sowing, I hear," said Mr. Hanson.

"I hear that the Torbersons bought an organ," said Torval.

"On time, no doubt. A nickel down and a dollar a month," said Mr. Hanson.

"You can do that?" said Torval. "Get it now and pay later?"

"Some new fangled business scheme developed by those Sears and Roebuck fellows."

"Are we sowing today," said Hans.

"You can haul a load of corn today, then make arrangements to swap the old buggy for a newer one."

"Too wet for seeding anyway," said Hans.

"And Swilley needs someone to fix his windmill."

"Me. Me." piped up Torval. "I helped him with it last fall."

"Enough business. Breakfast is on the table," said Carrie.

The Hanson clan tucked into the platters of ham and eggs, toast and jam set out on the scrubbed wooden table.

Later Hans dropped Torval off at the Swilley farm on his way to town.

"You'll have to walk home, brother. Don't work too hard."

"Just wait till I get my wheels. You'll eat my dust."

"Keep an eye on the weather. Looks unsettled."

~~~

By the time Torval had the gear train on the windmill greased and free of debris the sky had blackened with a long line of thunderheads. Would it be snow or driving rain was the only question as the temperature hovered just below the freezing point.

"Good thing it isn't any warmer, boy," said Mr. Swilley. "Warmer and we'd have a tornado sure."

"I'm almost finished. Give that cable a pull."

When the windmill creaked into action, Mr. Swilley handed Torval two greasy dollar bills and sent him on his way. Torval was soaked through and shivering when he burst through his own front door.

"Yikes! That's earning a buck the hard way," said Hans. "Maybe we better have a look at those bikes."

So Torval, wrapped in an old gray blanket, sat in front of the fire sipping hot tea, while Hans paged through the bicycle section of the Sears catalog. Six pages of dreams.

"Here's one that's half price."

"A kid size probably," said Torval.

"No. It's a regular size bike. Ah. It only comes in the ladies style."

"How much?"

"$8.95 plus shipping. Are we within 500 miles of Chicago? Yes? Then it's another 75 cents for a whopping total of $9.70."

"What about the boy's bike?"

"Says here the Gent's Kenwood is $10.95 on sale. The Napoleon is $15.75."

"Rats. I've got about $7.00."

"Maybe you can do the dollar down thing."

"Papa would kill me."

"Umm. Says you can't even do C.O.D. on bikes. Guess they're afraid you'll ride off into the wilderness without paying."

Torval leaped up, groaned and pretended to tear out his hair in frustration. Thoughts of attaining his cherished goal crumpled around his feet with the damp blanket. He paced back and forth muttering about being sentenced to a lifetime of wet hikes across the open prairie, long waits in dingy train stations, and worst of all—bumpy, knee-jarring horseback rides to hell and back. Hans watched his brother's show for a few minutes, then grabbed him by the shoulders and sat him down.

"Hey, hey, king of the melodrama," said Hans. "Maybe I can help."

"You'd loan me money?" said Torval. He looked up at Hans with his best attempt to look pathetic.

"Well. Maybe not loan. More like I'd buy your soul, you little tweak."

"For $2.70 you'd own me?"

"That's right, kid. Lock, stock, and barrel. At me bidding you'd be."

"For how long?"

Hans refused to answer, so Torval could only assume the smirk of glee on his brother's face boded ill for the future. Still, the temptation of a bright new bike crowded out any reservations he might have had. And, who knows, maybe Hans would spring for the more expensive model.

"We'll wire the order next time we're in town," said Hans. "Now go wash up for supper. Not a word of this to Papa, mind you, or the deal is off."

A few days later opportunity knocked in the form of a message that Hans was to take delivery of the new buggy that day.

"Well. Little brother. Looks like we have a job to do in town today," said Hans. "You don't need him here, do you Papa? The worthless brat still has the sniffles."

"Go, but stay out of trouble, mind you."

"I'll make a list of things we need," said Mrs. Hanson. No point in wasting a trip."

When the boys headed out the door, Mr. Hanson slipped an envelope to Hans.

"The money to make up the difference in the price of the new buggy. See that you keep a tight grip on it."

"Yes, Sir."

When they got to town, Hans stopped at the dry goods store.

"Start on Mother's list, while I get this buggy trade over with."

"Can't we order the bike first?"

With a 'see you later, slave' Hans turned the horse around and clattered off. The old buggy creaked and groaned as if to emphasize the need for a new one. Torval stuffed the order form into his shirt and scuffed up the steps to the store.

March 29, 1900 Thursday. Ordered my bike from Sears. Hans told Papa he paid $20 boot on the new buggy when he paid $10. That made a $7.20 profit for Hans. Forced me to lie.

Church Building and a Birthday

In 1893 the women of Grand Valley met to organize The Grand Valley Ladies Aid to work for the furtherance of God's Kingdom on earth. And to provide a vehicle for their own social life.

The Grand Valley Lutheran Church was organized on July 10, 1894 when bylaws and officers were approved. The Reverend P.H. Tetlie of nearby Canton, South Dakota agreed to hold services every fifth Sunday in the Grand Valley school house. His salary was set at $125.00 a year. This set off a flurry of events aimed at building a church house to hold the collective soul of the Grand Valley community. By April of 1900 the building fund had grown to just over a thousand dollars, more than half of the projected goal. The basket social was one of the fund raising vehicles.

"Why so glum, Torval?' said Carrie.

"Baby brother's worried about the social. Afraid he won't get a decent meal."

"Am not."

"With all the money he's been making, he should be able to bid with the best of them," said Mr. Hanson.

"Well, it's for a good cause," said Mrs. Hanson.

"He's dead broke," said Hans.

Torval squirmed and glared at Hans. The bike had not arrived yet, but the enormity of his deception had been growing in his mind. Just how was he going to explain things when the evidence appeared on the doorstep. And though he had willingly finished Hans's chores as well as his own each evening, Hans continued to jab and taunt him. This was just too much.

"I did it. I ordered my bike. Bought and paid for. It'll be here next week."

"Without telling us?"

"What were you thinking?" Mr. Hanson smacked the table so hard the dishes rattled. "Going behind my back won't be tolerated in this house."

Torval started to blame Hans, then realized that not owning up to his crime was a greater sin. Father and brother united in one fierce wall of anger. Speechless, Torval bent his head and slogged through the rest of his breakfast. The toast had turned to cardboard and the oatmeal quivered dangerously in his stomach. He finally gave up, excused himself and went out to finish his chores.

The family left him to his misery until the day of the basket social when both Carrie and his mother passed him two quarters for the bidding. Carrie had told him to be good, along with the news that Papa was almost as angry at Hans. Almost, but not quite.

Avoiding Hans, Torval left early to walk to the school house where the social was to take place. The dry, boring hike along the dirt roads only reminded him of why he was in this mess. Soon he would be free of all this tedium and bother. His wheels, his graduation, maybe a job in town like Emil. Imagining himself an important person telling others to follow his bidding, made the time pass more quickly. By the time he reached the school house he was whistling.

Others from the senior class joined him and they soon had the school room arranged for the social. Tables, chairs, and benches set out in small groups with one long table at the head of the room for the baskets. When the girls arrived, they added bright table cloths and vases of flowers to complete the festive look.

The bidding was brisk and several young men outdid themselves in the challenge to share a basket with a certain young lady. Though the baskets were supposed to be anonymous, unmarked, many a hint or clue had been whispered beforehand. Torval had no special girl and simply bid his fifty cents on each basket. In the end he procured a rather plain one with a frill of yellow gingham and a daisy peeking out from under the tea towel covering its contents.

When he went forward to pick up his supper, Sarah Ulberg joined him and they found a space at one of the tables to spread out the contents of the prize. Though he knew Hans would tease him later, Torval found himself enjoying the shy girl and her offering of homemade pasties.

"My ma makes these," he offered. "Says they remind her of the old country."

"Mine too." said Sarah. "She helped me with the dough, but I did the rest."

~~~

April 6, 1900 Friday. Attended Basket social at G.V. I rec'd Sarah Ulberg's basket. Cost 50 cts. The net proceeds amt to 43 dols. Hattie Flory's basket received the highest price, $3.15.

~~~

Torval handed up another strip of wallpaper, then guided its lower edge into place as Hans aligned the top. Kneel on the floor to trim the excess, apply the glue with a wide brush, balance on the short ladder to hand off the paper, climb down, stoop to align the design, then burnish the paper flat. How many times had he done that today, Torval wondered. During a short break he looked around the living room and tried to count the strips. A dozen for the short walls, four times that for the long ones. Add that to the two bedrooms and wasn't even dinner time yet.

From his perch on the top of the long ladder Hans flicked wallpaper paste down on his brother's head.

"If that girl of yours could see you now."

"She's not my girl." Torval replied, way too vehemently. Belatedly he realized his tone conveyed his hope.

"You never know, Romeo. Maybe she wants her kitchen papered."

"You bugger."

Torval scooped up a fistful of the slimy paste, prepared to blast Hans.

Before he could launch it Mrs. Hanson appeared in the doorway flicking her dish towel and warning them of their papa's return.

"That was close," muttered Hans. "Let's get this last strip out of the soaking pan and pasted up."

The following Monday was Torval's birthday, but the day was consumed with finishing the papering and cleaning up the mess. By the time the floors were scrubbed and waxed, the last of the tools put away, and a last load of work clothes washed and put out to dry, everyone staggered off to bed, exhausted.

Torval lay awake on the narrow bunk under the eaves and wondered if his bike would ever arrive. Would he ever get away from Hans and what about a girl. He knew he really didn't care about Sarah. She was probably willing to be his girl, but he couldn't see himself with her long term. Time seemed an endless roll of gloom and doom.

~~~

April 10, 1900 Tuesday. They remembered my birthday a day late. 19 yrs and 1 day old. Rec'd $1 as a present from Ma.

April 13 1900 Friday. Crucifixion day services-by Rev Tetlie at G.V.S.H.

Even endless waiting has an end though and Torval survived the wallpapering, his forgotten birthday, Easter Sunday at the Grand Valley Church, and three days of chores and scolding.

Mr. Hanson put down his fork when Torval made for the front door for the umpteenth time. "You're wearing a path to the mail box, boy."

"Sorry." Torval slumped back down in his chair.

"Don't you think we've punished the boy enough? It's not like he's stolen something," said Mrs. Hanson.

Torval watched to see if anyone noticed Hans's guilty blush, but it seemed to pass unnoticed in the rush to finish breakfast.

School seemed endless and even the buzz about moving graduation ceremonies to a larger, rival school failed to keep Torval's interest for long. He sprinted the mile home and arrived hot and winded. He thought he had suffered needlessly, when Hans popped out from behind the house wobbling like crazy on the new bike. He swooped past Torval and sent a spew of dirt into the air.

"Looky, looky little brother," taunted Hans. "See what we got."

"We? Get back here. It's mine!"

Hans careened down the road, barely able to avoid the ditches on either side with Torval running behind threatening mayhem. Looking back to jeer at Torval one more time, Hans barely missed a big rock only to smack into the mailbox. He flipped over the handlebars and tangled in the barb wire fence. The bike coasted a few more feet, then clattered over on its side in the grass.

Torval ran to pick up the bike, wipe the dirt from its frame and fenders, check for dents and damage. When he found the bike intact, he turned to Hans who was groaning and thrashing about on the ground in splendid theatrical fashion.

"Help me, Squirt. Don't just stand there gawking."

"Serves you right," growled Torval. He laid the bike down gently and went to help. "Stop kicking. Your pants are caught in the fence. Oh, oh, ripped too."

Freed from the fence, Hans examined the mail box. "Damn, it's pretty smashed. Pa will have our hide."

"Your hide," corrected Torval. "And don't let Ma hear you swear like that."

"I don't know what you see in that bike. Give me a good horse any day."

Hans dusted himself off and headed for the barn. Torval was too absorbed to mark the end of his serfdom.

April 17, 1900 Thursday. My bike arrives. Hans got in trouble.
April 18, 1900 Friday. I took a spin out west on my 2 wheels.

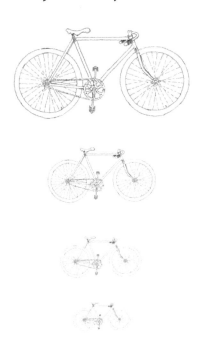

Graduation: Toil, and Celebration

The rest of April passed with less intense events. Work commenced on the sewers at Canton; Torval's brother Emil finished his course at business school; hogs were selling for $5.00 a hundred—a nickel a pound.

May began on a Monday and school was dismissed so the students could spread out across the prairie leaving May baskets at the various farm homes. Torval, dressed in women's garb, and Sarah, wearing old bibbed overalls, left pert paper cones filled with spring wild flowers on door knobs. After a quick knock on each door they fled to the bushes to watch the homeowner examine the prize.

Eighty acres of land sold for $2,400, corn was planted, barn building commenced, and a number of families planned trips to visit their homeland of Norway.

The Seventeenth of May was another holiday. This time in celebration of Norway's Freedom Day, the day that country achieved its independence from Sweden. Called 'Syttende Mai,' it was marked by children's parades, marching bands, flag waving and food. Hans, Torval, and Carrie went with their parents to nearby Augustana College to picnic and listen to the music. Another sign that on the prairies of 1900 grown children were firmly planted in the family unit until they married.

By the end of May Torval was proficient enough in the art of bicycling to make the trip into town. He had been riding the mile to school for a month and the excitement had worn off.

"How was town, wheel man," asked Hans at breakfast Monday morning.

"Jumping. The delegates from the State convention came in on the noon train."

"Did they decide in the favor of that Roosevelt fellow," asked Mr. Hanson.

"Roosevelt's a Republican, Papa," said Carrie. "This was the convention in Sioux Falls."

"The Populist Party. They want to merge with the Democrats. They nominated William Jennings Bryan."

"I thought they nominated Wharton Barker and that Ignatius Donnelly fellow."

"That was the mainstream Populists," said Torval. "This was the Fusion Faction."

"Land's sake. It sounds like a lot of fiddle faddle," said Mrs. Hanson. "How can you keep it all straight?"

Torval grabbed another piece of toast and pushed back from the table. "Zach Billow made a speech from the train platform. Says this will be a new era if we elect Bryan." He declared he was late for school and bolted from the room.

~~~

On Monday May 28, 1900 there was a partial eclipse of the sun that lasted over two hours. Torval skipped school to go fishing with friends. Wednesday was Decoration Day, a school holiday that included a visit to the cemetery for prayers and speeches. The day ended with a party that went on until dawn.

On Thursday graduation ceremonies were held at Bethlehem Church for the slightly groggy and somewhat hung over crowd of seniors. Torval, dressed in his Sunday suit, received his diploma with the glee usually reserved for calves let out of the pen to romp in green pastures.

~~~

June may have been seen as a big let-down by some of the students, but for Torval it was a re-birth. He found he was interested in all manner of things going on in the neighborhood and in town. Anything to avoid farm work.

"Are you off to town again, Boy?"

"Yes, sir, I've finished my chores. I won't be long."

"See that you're back in time for supper."

"Can you pick up a card of buttons? Here's the one to match," said Carrie. She handed Torval a button and a quarter.

"Since you're going anyway, I need blue thread," said Mrs. Hanson.

"At your service, ladies." Torval collected samples and two quarters, then headed for the door.

"Use the change for yourself," whispered Carrie as she followed her brother outside. "If you see Sarah, buy her an ice cream."

In town Torval made his purchases at the dry goods store, then joined a crowd of people watching several peddlers tout their wares. One ragged fellow attracted attention by juggling three long necked bottles while he sang bits of opera. Another insisted his wares would cure any disease known to man or beast. Torval watched a few minutes, then moved on to a young man with an array of mechanical toys that jigged and walked about on his folding table.

This swarm of peddlers descended on the county every spring. Some drove dusty buggies with weary horses, other came on foot with their wares slung over their shoulders. Most were young Jewish boys, newly immigrated, trying to learn the language and make a place for themselves in the world.

Torval examined the drumming bears and twirling clowns before he saw a less exotic contraption at the back of the peddlers table.

"What's this?" he jabbed his finger at a mess of wires and cog wheels. "Does it do something?"

"Not yet. Working on it."

"It has a battery?"

"I hope to build it into this toy carriage. Make the battery run the wheels."

"Can it move the horse's legs too?"

"Maybe. If I can figure out the gearing."

Torval wandered off without buying anything, his mind working at the problem of powering machines with something other than muscle—man or beast.

One of Torval's classmates accosted him. "Have you heard there's the party at Billers next week?"

"Sounds good. I'll be there."

"Has the census taker been to your place yet?"

"Yes. Mr. Queen came by yesterday. Asked about a million questions."

"Crops look good this year. Bout time for wheat harvest. How's your corn doing?"

"Okay, I guess. It's green anyway. Say, there's a party at my uncle's place tomorrow night. Consider yourself invited."

"See you then."

~~~

June 10, 1900 Sunday. Picnic at O. Qvedt's near river. Dance in Mikelson's barn at dawn of day.

June 11, 1900 Monday. Party for Miss Birdie Whitehead at Billers. Just a fine time.

June 13, 1900 Wednesday. Mickelson's barn finished, cost total $350. Party into the wee hours. The grain has headed.

~~~

After a few weeks of watching Torval head out to socialize every night and drag himself out of bed the next day Mr. Hanson broke his silence. "Are you about ready to get back to work, boy?"

"Yes, Papa, soon," said Torval. "Carrie asked me to carry some quilts to the school house for the Aid Society sale."

"That's not work."

"Sale is next Wednesday. I'm supposed to cashier."

"Hans needs help with that section fence by the creek. See that you're down there bright and early. Vacation is over."

Torval did manage to salvage his time at the Aid Society sale before the world of manual labor glommed onto him for real.

June 27, 1900 Wednesday. Aid Society sale. Proceeds netted 74 dollars. 3-4 weddings on this date.

Torval spent the first few days of his work sentence plowing sections to be planted with late corn. Long days guiding a slow team of horses back and forth, round and round in endless repetition. With the plowing and seeding over he was soon knee deep in the barley harvest, then the winter wheat was ready. He tried to concentrate on the fact that wheat was selling at an all time high of 70 cents a bushel and the year's yield was good. He passed the time calculating how much money each odd shaped field might yield and found he despised the work less when he could imagine the grain as money.

Still, with the vigor of youth he managed to attend several more summer weddings, the South Highland County Aid sale, and the horse races at Canton. All without raising his father's ire.

July arrived hot and dry and though work seemed to occupy every waking moment, an undercurrent of excitement about the Fourth of July celebrations pervaded the atmosphere. The day dawned clear and dry.

"Are you riding that contraption of yours to town or are you coming with us, Torval?"

"Of course he'll take his bike." Hans finished washing up. "Bluster head rides that thing everywhere. He'll probably sprout wheels before long."

"Breakfast is on the table," said Carrie. "Did anyone feed the chickens?"

After a hasty meal Hans and his father went to harness the team. Torval helped carry the dirty dishes to the sink, then slipped out to polish his bike and check its tires and chain.

~~~

The entrance to the fairgrounds was clogged with vehicles when Torval arrived, but he managed to weave through the bottle-neck and shoot out into the grassy park with little delay. He joined a group of town boys who were arguing the merits of their bikes.

"Hey there, Hanson. Wot's that you're riding?"

"James, my man," acknowledged Torval. "Looks like you could use some fender work."

"Needs more than that, if you ask me," said a younger boy wheeling a red racer across the grass.

"Is that thing fast?" said Torval.

"Fast as blazes. Beat you fat heads any day."

"We'll see about that. Let's wait till Lute and Amos and their gang gets here and do this right. Heats and such."

"Maybe we can use the race track when the horses are done."

"I'll ask me dad. He's in charge of the grounds."

They agreed to meet later for a spectacular test of speed and agility. Torval pedaled off to meet up with the rest of his family who had claimed a spot under one of the old oak trees that dotted the grounds.

Several rounds of fried chicken, baked beans, and apple pie later the brothers pushed back from the table.

"Got to run. I'm helping set up for the dance," said Hans. He dusted off his shirt front and gave his mother a peck on the cheek. "Thanks for a great meal."

"Carrie did most of it."

"Nonsense. I don't have your touch with the beans. and your pie crust could win a blue ribbon any day."

"Always tastes better outside. Maybe it's the fresh air."

While the women gabbed about the food, Torval slipped away to join the mob of boys arguing the merits of their bikes. They paid scant attention to the horse races and displays of fancy rope tricks in front of the grandstand. After some experimenting they set up an obstacle course to show off their prowess. At first they were content to pedal through a winding series of poles on level ground, then two older boys routed the course through some rutted waste ground.

"Ouch. I can't ride this ground. Makes me bum hurt."

"Hard on the tires, for sure."

"Put it back the way we had it."

"Pansies. Show 'em, Duke. Show these namby pambies how to ride."

Duke obliged by shooting around the course, zigzagging back and forth to bounce off the biggest mounds of dirt, flying over the ruts with ease, and coming to a stop on his rear wheel.

"Not fair. His legs are longer."

"Yeah. And his bike is different."

"A trick bike, that's what it is."

"Ain't. It's just a plain old bike. Coward."

"Practice and nerves of steel, that's wot it takes, children," said Duke. "Let's go find a challenging place to ride. Leave the babies to this baby course."

Duke and the older boys rode off.

"Good riddance. Now we can fix our course back."

"Wait. Let me try it," said Torval. "Can't be that hard."

He snugged his pant legs tight with bike garters, wiped his hands dry, and straddled his machine. After a couple of practice whirls through the first two markers he headed for the uphill slope at full speed. Bent over the handle bars, legs pumping, friends cheering, Torval churned through dried grass and dirt up the slope. At the lip of the small hill his wheels went airborne and for one brief instant he felt weightless, exhilarated, master of all. The next instant he was spitting dirt and untangling himself from the wreckage of his bike.

July 4, 1900 Wednesday. 4th celebrated in grand style at home city of Canton. Barn dance principal feature. Tore up my wheels.

~~~

Torval limped around the house for a day. His split lip oozed and his bruises purpled out in fine fashion. Sympathy was in short supply. Even his mother paid him scant attention. The embarrassment of dragging his bike back to the wagon amidst the jeers of the older boys and the stares of the girls had been topped only by the reception he got from Hans and his father. Worst was looking at his crumpled bike. He was not yet up to figuring out how to repair it, so he stowed it in the barn out of sight.

July 5, 1900 Thursday. Windy, sleepy etc. G.V. school house is being painted.

July 6, 1900 Friday. Finished corn plowing. Good bye.

Saturday morning found the brothers hard at work cleaning and greasing wagons, repairing harness, and sweeping out grain bins in anticipation of the approaching oat harvest.

"You got that thing fixed yet?" said Hans. "Your wheels, I mean."

"Working on it," said Torval. "The frame needs a little straightening and I could use a couple of new spokes."

"Let's take it over to Torkelsons after we finish here. He has a big vise."

Just before supper they loaded the bike and drove the mile and a half to the neighboring farmstead. With a few words and a nod to the farmer they hauled the bike into the shed and finagled it onto the work bench. A few well chosen blows with a heavy mallet and the bike regained its proper shape.

"That should do it. A little paint and she'll be good as new."

"Thanks, Hans." Torval sighted down the bike's center. "I was afraid it was a total loss."

~~~

The summer continued hot and dry. The harvest kept everyone busy. Oats, barley, and wheat moved from field to barn to market in town where a stream of rail cars hauled it east to various mills. Hay was cut, hauled and pitched into the lofts of the huge barns across Lincoln County. The thermometer topped out near 98 degrees everyday. Torval spent all his waking hours driving the dusty road to the granaries in Canton. When he wasn't hauling grain for his father, he hired out to the neighbors. At 63 cents a bushel it was imperative to make every daylight hour count.

Still, there was time for an ice cream social at the Thompson place. Babies were born and a traveling Wild West show stopped in town on its way east. The South Dakota legislature funded an Indian Asylum to be built in Canton and the campaign for president rolled on.

July 27, 1900 Friday. My wheels repaired.

July 28, 1900 Saturday. Took a turn to town on bike. Time 20 minutes. Small show operating at Canton. Auction sale of broncos $55.00 and up.

Storm Clouds

August arrived hot and dry. Good for hay and harvest, bad for the struggling corn crop and kitchen gardens. House wives saved every drop of waste water for thirsty beans and cucumbers.

"Someone needs to go to the Widow Langs place this morning. Haul her barley to town. Torval?"

"Send Hans."

"She don't pay a fig. Let Wheel Head do it."

"There's a loaf of new bread for her. Take it along."

"Why me," said Torval. "It's always me that gets the crappy jobs."

Still grumbling Torval snatched up the bread and walked out. A whole day wasted, jolting along behind a sweating team of horses, eating dust, he thought. Dull, dull, dull.

~~~

Though the day had started with bright sun and absolute calm, the sky had turned dark by the time Torval delivered the last load of grain to the mill. Odd twinges of yellow edged the clouds on the horizon and the stillness seemed to have a voice that rose above the continual chittering of the prairie insects. The team pawed the ground eagerly when he turned them towards home.

The horses trotted briskly, heads up, snorting at bits of paper blowing across the road. Though it was barely 4:00 o'clock it was nearly dark by the time Torval reached Burke Road. He pulled up the team and sat listening for a minute. It was dead still. The birds and insects had ceased their harping. Even the horses stood quiet, heads up, ears cocked. The yellow tinged, green clouds were lower, heavier. As Torval watched they bunched and piled and swelled until angry cloud filled the entire western sky. When tiny black objects flying up into the cloud revealed themselves as barn siding, he jerked the team into action and spurted down the section road towards home. Rain fumed out of the black.

With the horses running full out he pulled into his own barn lot a few minutes later. Hans appeared through the pouring rain, a slicker over his head. It whipped about ineffectually before the wind caught it and whirled it away.

"Head for the cellar." The words tore away after the slicker.

"The team?"

"Unhitch them."

"In the barn?" asked Torval. "Is it safe?"

"No. Let them into the big pasture. They can shelter under the creek bank."

"Hurry, hurry. Thompson's barn went a few minutes ago."

Stripped of their harness, the team bolted into the rain. Torval and Hans pushed against the wind to the cellar entrance where their father dragged them down to safety.

"Gore, it's a bad one," said Hans. "Thought Wheelhead would blow away sure."

August 17, 1900 Tuesday. The biggest rain that has fallen for some years. Tornado winds. Thompson barn blows to the road. Pete Miller returns from Norway.

August 18, 1900 Wednesday. Another big rain, delay with harvesting.

~~~

When the storm passed, everyone emerged from the cellars to assess the damage. Debris cluttered the fence rows and stacked itself against tree trunks and buildings. The wind had tattered a number of sheds. Roof shingles littered the prairie. The biggest casualty was the Thompson barn which now sat slaunchwise across the road where it would remain, forcing traffic to detour through the nearby field, until November. The crops were unharmed and no one had been injured. Harvest continued.

On the Hanson farm wheat averaged 15 bushels to the acre, oats 35. August temperatures and a long dry spell gave the area a huge hay crop as well. When the hay was cut, stacked, and hauled to the barn on the Hanson farm, the workers moved to a neighboring farm where the farmer was side lined by illness.

Sundays offered some relief from the monotony of labor. Torval made the trip into Canton for a community picnic, then attended a horse sale the following weekend.

Broncos were brought in off the prairie to be auctioned. The unbroken animals were herded into the corrals at the fairgrounds. With large crowds watching an individual horse was sorted from the herd and the excitement began. A gang of men and boys grappled with the animal until it was saddled and blind folded. An intrepid volunteer mounted the explosive beast and the bucking contest began. While the horse and rider pair careened about the arena, the auctioneer rattled off his spiel to the buyers. By the time the horse was brought to a sedate walk or the rider was on the ground spitting dirt, the animal sold to the highest bidder.

August 25, 1900 Saturday. Broncos sold at Canton, great excitement in catching them.

~~~

Before Torval noticed, summer was replaced by the shorter days of autumn. He was disgusted with himself. How could he let valuable time slip by like that? All his plans forgotten in the frantic days of harvest. And it wasn't over. Ahead loomed more haying, getting the fat hogs to market, machine repair, cleaning, painting. Plowing for the winter wheat crop would soon commence, followed by harrowing and sowing. And now Hans was talking about working his future father-in-law's place. Who even knew Hans had a girl? wondered Torval. With Hans away the load would pass to Torval and Carrie. More and more he thought his brother Emil had made the right decision when he elected to go to business school.

"That doesn't look like a wagon axel, boy." said Mr. Hanson.

"Just greasing my bike chain. Tighten it up a link, too." Torval scrambled up from his seat on the big tool box. "I'll get to that axel in a minute."

"That wagon should be in the field by now."

"Okay. Now, I'll do it now."

"See that you do. We need to have a little talk. Tonight. After supper."

~~~

Torval paced about the parlor waiting for his father. I haven't been in here since cousin's Baine's funeral, he thought. More than a year ago. Straight-back chairs marched down one side of the room. Crocheted doilies sat primly on the overstuffed sofa facing them. No speck of dust ever dared rest on the polished tables and China figurines placed just so about the dim room. What was he in for anyway? Punishment was meted out in the kitchen or, worse, the barn. This meeting in the parlor was outside Torval's experience. He was still mulling this development when the door opened.

"What are we going to do with you, Torval?"

"Papa?" Torval stopped pacing and concentrated on a beaded lampshade just past his father's shoulder.

"I've been talking to your Uncle, James." said Mr. Hanson. "Well, sort of your uncle. He's my half-brother, in Sioux Falls."

"I don't remember him."

"Seemed to have your problem. Anything to get out of an honest day's work."

"Sir?" Torval cringed a bit. Was it that obvious?

"James has a general store and manages a sheep operation. Says he can use you."

"I hate sheep."

"In the store, boy. Stocking, inventory, sales."

Torval pulled his shoulders back and looked at his father.

"He'd send his boy here," continued Mr. Hanson. "Sort of a trade."

"Maybe he'll like farming."

"The boy has been in trouble. Fighting, gambling. Too many bad influences in the city."

"When do I go?"

"James will provide room and board. Your bicycle will be useful in the city. He thinks you can pick up a little extra cash doing deliveries."

"Is Hans really getting married?"

"Your mother isn't well. Don't put any extra work on her. Carrie can get your clothes in order."

"Will he stay here?"

"Pack your stuff and clean your room. You can leave after the Arneson wedding."

No More Windmill Repair

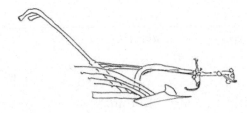

Or Plowing

Big City Life

Torval's move to Sioux Falls was put off a few weeks when he was invited on an excursion to Madison. The 390 mile round trip billed for the large sum of $3.50, but free passage was offered to a group of young people to help advertise the new sight-seeing rail journey. It was too good to pass up.

He returned in time to help with the removal of the Thompson barn from the road. An all night party celebrated the event. The following day Torval slipped away from the harvesters and pedaled into town for a baseball game between the Flandreau Indians and the Sioux Falls Nine.

A political rally for William Jennings Bryant drew him away from the threshing for a day. A picnic at the river to greet the new steamer Queen caused him to miss another day. A send off party for a group of Norwegians returning to their homeland delayed him once again. He cycled home in the wee hours with a full moon over his shoulder. Whistling a few bars of 'Casey Jones' he wheeled into the yard and leaned his bike against the garden fence. Two long strides and he gained the porch.

"What the hay?" he said. "My stuff."

Two fat satchels sat in front of the door with an envelope on top. He tried the door, but found it locked. "By gor. Who even knew you could lock it."

The envelope contained the 60 cent fare to Sioux Falls and a see you at Thanksgiving note. A post script in his mother's spider hand told him that Jack had arrived and needed his room.

~~~

After a sleepless night spent walking his bike back to Canton, his belongings balanced over the cross bar, Torval made the train to Sioux Falls. He soon settled in to city life and his new family. He liked the small lean-to room with its iron bedstead and private entrance. It had taken him a few days to digest the fact that 'Uncle Jim's' general store was mostly a drug store with a section of canned goods, hardware, paint, and ladies hats.

"Your eggs, Torv. Toast is on its way."

"Thanks, Aunt Ellen," said Torval.

"El, just plain 'El.' We don't stand on ceremony in this house."

"Got that, Torv? Jim and El. That's us," said Jim.

"Are you a real pharmacist?"

"You bet. I studied through a mail order class in the pharmaceutical arts and got my state license."

"I thought you needed to apprentice?"

"Most people go that route, but it takes longer. And the schools all require a year of high school."

"Only a year?"

"They're thinking of changing that to two years soon."

"You're lucky. You finished high school. Our generation mostly did the sixth grade, then went to work." El brought more toast. "Of course you don't learn millinery arts at most schools anyway."

"Millinery?" said Torval.

"Hat making. I'm a pretty fair seamstress too."

"Emil went a year to business school after high school," said Torval.

"He must have a good head for figures. I'd be bored with that stuff."

"Eat up, Torv. I'm sure Jim has plenty of work lined up for you today."

"As long as it doesn't involve mud or manure, I'm fired up and ready."

~~~

Torval soon found he was to be the dog's body in residence. He spent his first morning shifting boxes from one side of the store room to the other while Jim made notes about their contents. Finished, Jim instructed him to shuffle them back to their original places. Dusting shelves and arranging empty vials in 'just so' rows took up the afternoon. After supper El took over.

"If you got a minute, Torv, I can use your help." She led him to the parlor. "Sit."

Jim stood in the doorway and watched while El draped a swath of fabric over Torv's shoulders.

"Chin up, now." She fitted a band some stiff material around his head and pinned it. More material followed, then a felt crown and straw brim that swept up in front. Ribbons, silk roses, bands of satin grosgrain, more pins, many pins.

"What do you think, Jim? Isn't this just the latest?" said El.

"Straight from Paris. Looks like a keeper," said Jim. "Mrs. Penny will love it."

While El finished her creation and Torval fidgeted, Jim sat down to read the newspaper.

"Do ladies actually wear these things," said Torval. "It's heavy. And it prickles."

"I'll cure the prickles when I finish it, but the weight will be about the same."

"Gore. What a life you city ladies live."

"Doesn't your mother wear hats?"

"My sister, Carrie, might like this thing. She's always fussing with clothes and hair and such."

"Hold real still now and I'll relieve you of your headgear," said El. She lifted the hat straight up off Torval's head and held her creation out for his inspection.

"Zowie. Looks like a pink explosion."

Jim looked up from his paper. "Better you, than me. The fair in Yankton starts this weekend. Are you going?"

"I could take the train."

"May as well. It's a good time and I won't need your head for a few days."

"Roosevelt is going to be in town for a speech tomorrow."

"The Populist are having a rally too," said Torval. "They have some good ideas."

"Well, I'll be glad when all this electioneering is over," said Ellen.

~~~

A sudden winter storm blew in from Canada wiping away any thought of fairs and rallies. Torval counted up his meager savings and asked for an advance on his wages to buy a top coat. He was majorly annoyed to find it cost him nearly as much as his bike. Still, he had to keep up appearances. And it was cold.

As voting day approached, the electioneering increased. Local candidates joined state hopefuls at a series of rallies, speeches on the court house steps, and a last minute railroad run through the state by representatives of the major national parties. All the hullabaloo culminated on November 6 with a landslide vote for McKinley. The people had spoken.

November 7, 1900 Wednesday. Swept and mopped the store floor this morning, it was dirty of course. Honored position indeed.

November 11, 1900 Sunday. I attend Congregational Church today. Wrote three letters to Lincoln County.

~~~

"Mail call," said Jim. "One for you, Torv. Guess somebody loves you after all."

"No electioneering handbills, I hope," said Ellen. "Glad that's over."

Torval recognized Carrie's flowing script on the pale lavender envelope.

"A girl?" said Ellen.

"My sister. She won the school penmanship medal."

"Well, what does she have to report?"

"Says everyone is fine. Jack is settling in well. Seems to like farming."

"That's a relief. I worry about that boy."

"Here's something." Torval sounded excited. "Bob Carmel and my cousin, Jake, bought a claim in the badlands."

"Bet those miserable bits of land are going cheap," said Jim. "No water."

"Nobody to bother you, tell you what to do," said Torval. "Good hunting, freedom."

"Snakes and Indians. Give me city life any day," said Ellen.

November 12, 1900 Monday. Cold, wintry day. Hope Jake and Bob are having fun with their new homestead.

~~~

""Get those boxes unpacked, Torv," said Jim. "Wool socks next to the counter. And put the Jenson Cough remedy right out front."

"Expecting a bad winter?"

"Always prepare for the worst. Or, in this case, the best for the store."

"Snow shovels, wool caps, gloves. Hey! Sleds. Good thinking."

"Folks can't spend all their time working. There's a case of playing cards in there somewhere. Line the sleds up along the walk out front."

"What's that," Torval ran for the door with Jim close behind.

Dust and noise filled the street as a team hitched to a light buggy spurted up the street. The buggy swayed and bumped precariously before it snagged the wheel of a freight wagon and turned over. On its side the wreck did little more than panic the team. The frenzied horses careened off the side of the newspaper building and disappeared down a narrow alleyway. Parts of the buggy flew everywhere.

"Get a couple of those buck knives, Torv," said Jim. "I'll grab some rope."

The intrepid pair ran down the alley after the runaway. They found the team hopelessly snared in Mrs. Penny's fence. One horse was down and in danger of being trampled by his teammate.

Jim threw his coat over the head of one frenzied horse and directed Torval to sit on the downed horse's head and start cutting harness. By the time the horses were freed from harness and fence a crowd had gathered and many willing hands soothed the animals, put Mrs. Penny's fence to rights, and hauled the broken buggy off to the livery barn.

"A job well done, Torv," said Jim. "No real harm done."

"Too bad we can't invent a steam buggy. Retire all the horses."

"I hear there's a fellow working on it."

"Can't happen soon enough to suit me," said Torval.

November 23, 1900 Friday. A runaway in town. No obstruction followed.

November 24, 1900 Saturday. Lots of turkeys raffled off for Thanksgiving. Party at Dr. White's.

November 25, 1900 Sunday. Attended Church of course today as usual, temperance service in the Congregational Church.

November 26, 1900 Monday. Nice weather. No sign of storm in the near future.

Abraham Lincoln had declared Thanksgiving a national holiday in 1863 and congress had mandated the last Thursday of November as the official date. Not until Roosevelt changed it in 1939 did the celebration move to the third Thursday of the month.

Unfortunately Torval's weather forecast missed a sudden storm out of Canada. By Wednesday the trains sat idle on their iced over rails, the farrier was kept busy replacing the shoes of slick shod horses with ice caulks, and walking was hazardous.

"Guess you're stuck with us this year," said Jim. "Hope Jack has sense enough to stay put."

"You can help with the turkey," said Ellen.

"There's a dance at the lodge hall in case you're interested."

"You bet. Thanks, Uncle Jim."

"A dance, Jim? Why would a young fellow be interested in a dance?"

"Girls, of course."

Torval had the good grace to blush.

November 29, 1900 Thursday. A large dance at the Hall to-night. The last dog was hung at 4 o'clock. We had a splendid time.

~~~

The Christmas season began with a progressive dinner that wound up with apple pie and thick cheddar cheese wedges at Jim and Ellen's house. Stuffed with courses of beet pudding, lutefisk, potatoes in cream sauce, roast lamb with mint, and many rounds of hot spiced apple cider and gallons of coffee the partiers settled down to play cards and sing carols.

A few days later Torval found another aspect of city life that interested him more than parties. Court was in session. Spectators welcome.

December 3, 1900 Monday. A snow today covering the earth with a white shirt.

December 4, 1900 Tuesday. Court convenes in Minnehaha County in the city of Sioux Falls. Commences with a dispute over a steer.

"Off to court again?" said Jim.

"If it's okay with you," said Torval. "I've swept up and unpacked that last shipment. I'll work extra this evening."

"No problem. You can learn plenty observing those lawyer fellows."

"Today should be the last session this year."

December 5, 1900 Wednesday. Court continues with a trial over a thirty dollar note. Court adjourns.

Ellen filled the milk pitcher and spooned out oatmeal. "There's brown sugar in the white bowl, jam coming up."

"Sit and eat, El. We can serve ourselves."

Torval piled toast on a serving plate and put it down in the middle of the table. He found the jam and a spoon, then sat down to eat.

"How was court?"

"Interesting. One fellow had borrowed thirty dollars. Signed a note, then refused to pay," said Torval. "It was an open and shut case. The judge admonished us to always get things in writing."

"Even with friends?"

"Especially with friends. And relatives."

"So he had to pay the money?"

"And he got five days in jail for attempted petty larceny. Judge said he had to learn. Plus he had done the same thing before."

"Got a little extra job for you today if you want it," said Jim.

"Sure thing," said Torval.

"McDonald, the meat market guy is moving his shop to Main Street. Needs a strong back and willing hands. He'll pay well."

"Thanks. I'll go over when I finish up in the store."

"Go now. I can do without you today. Time is money."

Torval soon found that what the meat man really needed was help organizing the new shop. Torval spent the day sorting trays, utensils, storage pans, and bins. While McDonald and his son did the heavy work, he worked up a system of signs and labels so the customer could see his choices at a glance along with the price. By the time all the beef sides, ribs, and hams were stowed in the ice room the shop looked as if it had always been there.

December 6, 1900 Thursday. Weather is clear and pleasing to my taste. McDonald's meat market moved.

December 7, 1900 Friday. Small snow storm this morning. Social at Shober's. Card party a Jim and El's.

December 11, 1900 Tuesday. Fair. Storm in eastern portions. No dance tonight.

~~~

Ellen and Torval swathed the store with evergreens, then added red bows and silver stars. Jim held the ladder and gave out free advice between customers. The fear of a flu epidemic and widespread cases of sniffles and sore throat had a steady stream of people braving the weather in search of remedies. Cough medicine was a top seller.

"Guess you'll be heading home for Christmas before long," said Jim.

"Big party in Canton the Saturday before. Sort of a Grand Valley reunion."

"Take the train to Canton after work. Party, then catch a ride home."

"Emil will be there. I'll go with him."

"Maybe Jack will come home," said Ellen.

"Don't count on it. He's talking about heading west again."

December 12, 1900 Wednesday. Commencing to get ready for the holiday trade at the store of J.M. Hanson of Sioux Falls, S.Dak.

66

CANTON

~~Klara~~

By the end of her first week at the home of old Missus Ulner Klara learned of a position in Canton, a small neighboring village.

"It pays good," said Mr. Rand. "The Lawrences are particular about their boys and want a young, energetic nanny."

"I'm much obliged," said Klara. "How far is it?"

"They sent a train ticket. You can go in the morning."

New Job, New Home
~~~

Klara had not yet ceased to marvel at her sudden good fortune. She felt like singing as she tidied the nursery. Rows of neatly folded shirts and britches with a few sailor suits and caps stared back at her from the shelves of the huge wardrobe. Boxes of alphabet blocks and windup toys waited on the lower shelves. With her duster in hand she peeked in at the two little boys napping in the alcove off the playroom.

The Christmas tree in the corner filled the room with the aroma of a spruce forest and filled Klara's heart with a momentary ache for home. But then, her joy in the ornament laden tree presiding over the nursery playroom banished her homesickness almost as soon as it arrived.

Except for Sophia's mean, cramped walkup in New York Klara had never been inside an American home before Mrs. Lawrence had rescued her. The spacious rooms and high ceilings made her feel like dancing. And the light. The light poured in through the wide windows and reflected off the white walls and lace curtains into her very soul.

She banished stray thoughts of the night she had been abandoned and robbed by her friends in the dismal flophouse in Sioux Falls by concentrating on the task of sorting and polishing the boys' shoes and boots. How amazing to know people with more than one pair, new and unpatched with matching store bought socks. And children at that. What must Mrs. Lawrence's wardrobe contain. It made Klara's head spin.

Her own room was a marvel. Her own room. She savored the words. Two windows overlooking the garden and a feather bed. Walls covered with pale rose paper, a soft rug, a closet bigger than her bed. She smiled at the thought of that closet. When Mrs. Lawrence first showed it to her, Klara thought it was to be her bedroom so she set about trying to fit her trunk in sidewise to give her room to stretch out on the floor. Mrs. Lawrence laughed until the tears came when she figured out what Klara had been thinking.

With the thought that the boys would be awake soon Klara hurried to finish her chores. She set the low table with small plates and mugs, then hurried to the kitchen for the tea tray. The kitchen girl met her in the hall.

"All set, Miss," said Tillie. "New butter and fresh bread today. Jams not bad either. Plum."

She squeezed past Klara and placed the tray on the nursery sideboard. With a grand gesture she whipped the cloth from the tray and held it up to Klara.

"Towel," she exaggerated the word and pointed. "Towel."

She folded the linen cloth and started on the tray. Bound and determined to teach Klara English, she went through its entire contents.

"Bread, butter, butter knife, plum jam, milk, liverwurst.

Liverwurst before jam. Remember that. Napkins, tea cup, tea pot, cozy."

Pointing and mouthing words, she refused to relinquish the tray until Klara repeated everything she said. Finished with the names of the tea things, she decided to review the other objects on the side board, then went on to Klara's clothing. Only the sound of waking children put an end to the lesson.

Exasperated, yet pleased with herself, Klara pushed Tillie to the door.

"Kiddels up," she said.

"The children are awake," corrected Tillie. "Say it. Children, not kiddels."

Klara laughed and hugged her self-appointed teacher.

~~~

"Mail. Klara, you have a letter," said Mrs. Lawrence.

"Who can it be?"

"Comes from the old country by the look of it."

"Here, use my letter opener," said Mr. Lawrence. He passed the tiny sword to Klara and continued to sort through his own pile of mail. The entire family gathered for the mid-day meal including Klara and Tillie. The informal occasion often turned into a collage of sandwiches, mail, displays of the boys' latest drawings, newspapers, pots of tea, cookie crumbs, and spilled milk. Tillie said it was like cleaning up after pigs except that the pigs ate all the spilled food. Never-the-less, she joined in whole-heartedly and added to the mix with tales of her old life in the Smokey Mountains.

Klara took the envelope by one corner and peered at it intently. Thin and flat it bore the Smedjebacken postmark. The handwriting seemed vaguely familiar, but then, she reminded herself, I've never seen any of my family's writing except my brother's.

"It won't bite you, Klara," said Tillie. "Open it."

"She fears bad news," said Mrs. Lawrence. "It's old country superstition."

"It's probably just an answer to the letter you sent in November."

Mr. Lawrence took the envelope from her trembling fingers, slit the end, and pulled out a card with bright poinsettias.

"A Christmas card. Nothing to fear."

Klara scanned the brief message of good cheer on the card, then unfolded the thin square of paper inside the card.

Dear Klara,

We were so happy to get your letter. Why did it take you so long to write? We are about as usual. Naomi is getting so big. Stina and I have managed to attend school nearly everyday since September. The boys are into everything. Pappa is away at work in the mine at Ludvika. We hope he can come home for Christmas. Mamma is unwell, but refuses to see the doctor.

If you can find the time, I would like to know if there is work there for me. I can do most anything. Please let me know before the spring conscription for the army is announced.

Your loving brother,

Ivar

"So what does it say," said Tillie. "Is anyone dead?"

"My brother wants to find work here."

"How many brothers do you have?" said Mr. Lawrence.

"She has three," said Tillie. "Ivar, Will, and James."

"And which of these lads wants work?"

"Ivar, the oldest. He fears being forced into the army."

Later, when the children were safely asleep, Klara padded down the back stair to Tillie's room. When she found the room unoccupied, she back-tracked to the kitchen where she found Tillie on her hands and knees scrubbing the floor.

"Still working?"

"I don't sleep so good. Keep me company?"

"Can you help with my letter?"

So between dumping wash water, rinse water, and applying a high shine of wax on floor, they puzzled together a letter to Ivar. Neither Tillie nor Klara were very adept at writing and then, there was the problem of language. They finally decided to write in English and leave the burden of translation to the recipient. No wonder letters home were so short and far between. Klara gritted her teeth and added a post script in Swedish to wish her parents and other siblings well.

"There. All done," said Tillie.

"Do you think I can send a little money with it?"

"You actually have money?" Tillie seemed surprised.

Embarrassed, Klara admitted that she had saved nearly every penny of her pay including the money Mrs. Lawrence had given her for new socks and undies.

"Stars and garters, girl. Live a little. Buy you some pretties."

"Christmas. Am I to buy presents? For the family? You?" Klara was awash with embarrassment. "But there won't be any presents at home."

After Klara calmed down a bit, they decided to divide Klara's savings three ways. The larger portion went with Mr. Lawrence to be converted to a money order for Ivar. Klara knew he would use it fairly. The rest, promised Tillie, would more than cover presents and some new clothes for Klara.

"I don't know how you did it, girl," said Tillie. "Bought me the grandest pair of shoes with my first money. Did I ever feel flush."

Klara glanced at Tillie's feet.

"Not these clodhoppers. These be me work shoes."

"You have two pairs?"

"Six," said Tillie.

"Pappa made our shoes."

"They look it."

~~~

Though it was December, the weather felt more like late spring. The roads were dry and no predictions of winter storm circulated through Lincoln County. Mrs. Lawrence decided to take advantage of the respite with a trip to the city. She stopped by the nursery on her way upstairs. After tucking the boys in and giving each a kiss, she drew Klara aside.

"I'm taking the boys to visit their grandmother in Sioux Falls tomorrow."

"I'll have them ready," said Klara.

"I thought you and Tillie might like to come along. Grandmom Lawrence will send her hired man to pick us up at the station. He can drop you off downtown for some shopping and lunch. Tillie can show you around. We'll pick you up in time to catch the five o'clock train."

After a light snow fall in early December the weather had turned summery so Klara didn't bother with shawl or jacket when she left the house. The boys were spic and span in their sailor suits. Tillie, always the worry wort, wore a bonnet and gloves and carried a large handbag with who knew what to get her through the day in maximum comfort. Mrs. Lawrence teased her a bit, then turned her attention to keeping the boys clean and out of mischief.

Unlike the tiny burg of Canton, downtown Sioux Falls had paved streets and sidewalks. Buggies and bicycles seemed to be racing in every direction. The light poles and shop windows were decorated with greenery and ribbons.

After the first few shops Klara's head was over flowing with Tillie's chatter, images of all manner of goods, and endless decisions.

"Try these shoes," said Tillie. "They are so sweet."

Baffled, Klara tried to wedge her stockinged foot into the bow trimmed slipper. Did women actually wear these flimsy things. And how do they stay on.

"Oh, too small, Said Tillie. "Let me get the salesman."

Klara sat stiffly upright with the slipper hooked over her big toe, while Tillie disappeared into the back of the store. She tried to imagine herself standing in a tranquil forest picking ferns while other shoppers pushed and eddied around her. A small child sprawled in the seat next to her. He bumped up and down and pointed at her old homemade shoes.

"Mama, Mama. Lookie the funny shoes."

"Hush, Sam. It's not polite to talk about less fortunate people."

Mortified, Klara wanted to run out of the store. She looked around for Tillie, but, for once, could not spot her. By the time she did return several older children had joined in the teasing.

"Scat. Scat," Tillie sent them scurrying. "Where are your parents, anyway?"

"Can we leave now," whispered Klara. "I don't really need these."

"Nonsense." Tillie plunked down beside her friend. "The salesman is coming."

Klara hardly noticed when the salesman pronounced the next pair of shoes a perfect fit.

"Why, Miss, this Douglas strap sandal is suitable for street or dress up. See the McKay stitching. And the flexible sole. So comfy.

You can wear it dancing with your fellow. It will last for ages."

When Klara hesitated, he promised he could order it in the popular patent leather version for just forty-eight cents extra.

"No," said Tillie. "She'll take this pair."

Klara paid the eighty-five cent sale price and followed Tillie out to the street with her first major purchase.

"Now that was progress," said Tillie. "Your first real bargain."

"Bargain? What do shoes usually cost?"

"Oh, about twice what you paid. Now to get you some hose."

They looked at silk hose, fancy embroidered hose, and lace effect hose, all of which Klara adamantly rejected as being nearly as pricey as shoes and, besides, who would see them anyway.

"Your fellow, of course," said Tillie. "Look at these sweet things. Blue with white dots and flowers. And light weight cotton too. I be needing these myself."

"Twenty-six cents. Are you mad," said Klara. "These plain ones are nine cents."

"Here they are in red. Perfect with your new shoes."

In the end Klara came away with both a red pair and a blue pair along with six pair of the plain everyday hose. Tillie had two of each and an extravagant pair of imported silk stockings in ribbed black to boot.

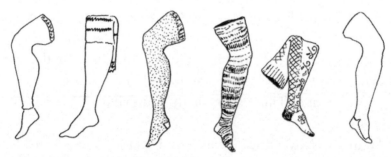

"Food, now we need food," chanted Tillie. "Let's lunch at the five and dime."

Seated on stools at the counter with their bundles at their feet, Klara and Tillie munched on toasted cheese sandwiches and eyed the dessert menu posted a few feet away.

"Presents for the boys," said Tillie. "Then a new outfit for you at Berg's."

"No more shopping. My head is spinning."

"You'll perk up."

"Never again."

"Well, at the least, we have to find something for the boys."

Klara shook her head, too weary to argue. She paid the counterman and followed Tillie to the toy aisles. A small truck and a stuffed bear joined the hose and shoes in her bag. Later, at the train station, Klara felt a small niggle of regret over her hasty decision. Maybe she should try harder to fit in and make herself less noticeable.

~~~

The Christmas dance party was to be held at the Grand Valley School house. One of Tillie's numerous beaus had invited her and she insisted Klara be included. Klara moaned about her lack of a suitable dress, her inability to dance, and would she know anyone there at all.

"You'll know me," said Tillie. "And Jack. You met him last week."

"What will I wear?"

"Now who's to blame for that you goose."

Tillie was thrashing through the frocks in her own closet when Mrs. Lawrence appeared.

"My, my," she said with mock severity. "All play and no work from the two of you."

"The boys are napping and I help Tillie with the kitchen so we get done quick like a scalded rabbit."

"Whatever," said Mrs. Lawrence. "I think I can help."

She led the girls upstairs to the box room and indicated an old wardrobe.

"There should be several suitable frocks in there. Help your selves. Be sure to put them back clean and tidy."

After much giggling Klara tried a rather severe gray dress with a straight skirt. It would fit with a few tucks to the waist, but Tillie declared it made her look like a frump and returned it to the wardrobe. A green satin frock was too frilly and Klara refused to even touch a frothy pink number with faux fur around the neck and hem.

"Red. Let me try the red one," said Klara. "So beauteous."

"Beautiful," corrected Tillie. "Maybe it will suit you."

The red silk fit. It was years out of style, but suited Klara perfectly. She twirled in a circle and posed for Tillie.

"You'll knock 'em dead, sister. Like something out of Harpers."

"You think? Is not too floozy?"

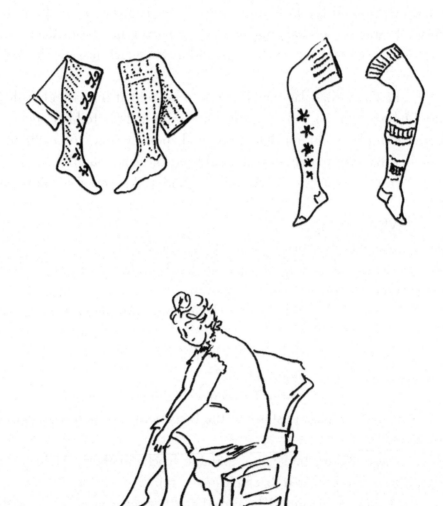

Dancing the Night Away

Festooned with pine boughs and red ribbon, tinsel and candy canes, the school house glowed in the light of dozens of oil lamps. A light dusting of snow added to the picture perfect scene. Jack delivered the two girls in a high top buggy borrowed from his uncle. The old team managed to step lively the last quarter mile and arrived at the door in fine style. Jack tossed the reins to a boy and handed Tillie and Klara out of the buggy, then escorted them to the door.

"I'll blanket the team. Meet you inside," said Jack. "See that Tillie doesn't get sassy with anyone while I'm gone."

"You dog, you," said Tillie. She grabbed Klara by the elbow and propelled her into the hall.

Jack made his entrance a few minutes later. He pushed a tall, skinny fellow ahead of him.

"Ladies. Meet my cousin, Torv. Found him skulking around the back door."

"No skulking," said Torval. "Just grabbing a smoke."

"I'm sleeping in his bed," said Jack with a suggestive wink. Seeing that he had properly horrified the girls, he continued, "That's all right. He's sleeping in mine. Our folks traded us. For our own good they said."

"How's that working out, Jack?" said Torval.

"Great. I like the farm. Wide open spaces. Pretty women." He put his arm around Tillie. Just before he whirled her away, he introduced Klara as Tillie's friend.

"He's a talker," said Torval. He steered Klara towards the refreshment table.

"So is Tillie. Never stops."

"Do you dance?"

"No. I never learn."

"Me either. Seems silly."

When Klara didn't answer, he asked how she knew Tillie, then where they worked. He soon discovered she had come over from the old country that spring and tried his second hand Norwegian on her. Klara asked how he knew the language which was so similar to her own Swedish and he told her his parents spoke it at home. Dancing was forgotten as they jabbered away. Klara told him about her family back home and her hope that her brother would come over by summer. Torv spoke of his brother's impending wedding and his new job in Sioux Falls. When Klara looked suitably impressed, he pumped up his position at the drug store with stories about accidents and epidemics where he had assisted his uncle the pharmacist who was almost a doctor. Soon they were settled in a comfy corner of the hall away from the crowd. When Torval reached for Kara's hand, she made no protest. When he kissed her, she kissed him back.

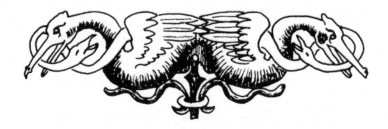

Dancing Dreams, Talking Horses

Promise and Pitfalls

The morning after the party at the school house Klara approached Tillie with some trepidation. Her head hurt and she felt shaky. Even her clothing felt odd against her skin.

"I must be getting sick," she told Tillie. "My head feels so tight."

"Did you try that stuff Jack was handing out?"

"Just a little," Klara said. "He seemed to expect it. I didn't want to be rude."

"Better rude than hung over. That brew of his is lethal."

"Alcohol?"

"You'll be fine in a couple of hours, but I'd stay away from the strong stuff if I was you. The Missus don't like strong drink or smoking either."

Klara threw herself down on the kitchen bench and howled.

"Hey. Hey. It's just a hangover. How bad can it be," clucked Tillie. "Pull yourself together."

"Not that," sobbed Klara. "I turn into my mother."

"Silly girl. I'll get you some chamomile tea. Settle your stomach."

"You don't understand."

Tillie snorted and retreated to the stove where she put the kettle to boil. She attacked the stack of dirty dishes while she waited. By the time she got to the pots and pans the kettle was singing. Klara had not moved an inch.

"Sit up and drink this," said Tillie. "Pull yourself together."

Klara sat up and accepted the offered cup. "Too hot."

"Put it down and explain about your mother," said Tillie.

Between sobs and sips Klara told stories about brannvin and her mother's painful need of it.

"What is this brannvin?"

"Bottled fire. The farmer folk make it from anything that will ferment. Grain, potatoes. They take food from the mouths of the kiddels to make drink."

"Well, you don't have to imbibe again," said Tillie.

Klara got up and assembled the breakfast tray for her young charges. She paused in the doorway. "Trouble is, Tillie, I liked it. I felt free."

~~~

The first real blizzard of the season preserved Klara from further temptation. The boys in her charge, cranky with being shut in and anxious for Christmas Eve, pestered her for games and stories. The howling wind and frigid temperatures kept her house-bound. Parties, sing alongs, and even church services were canceled as folks hunkered down to wait out the series of storms.

"What do you think Jack is doing right now?" Klara and the boys were making cookies under Tillie's tutelage.

"Slogging through the snow bringing water to thirsty cows, no doubt."

"Don't you worry?"

"He's a big boy."

"Our cow lived in the house," said Klara.

"What? Ridiculous."

"No, no. Not in same room. There was a little door from kitchen."

"Well, you won't catch me sleeping with a cow," said Tillie.

"Do you think Torval is bringing water to cows?"

"He's a city boy now. Snug in his shop selling potions to rich customers."

~~~

Had the girls only known, Torval was up to his eyebrows in frozen muck. Literally. He pressed his forehead against the cow's filthy side and pushed. When the animal refused to move, he gripped

Jim's hand under the cow's tail and the two of them struggled to get purchase on the slippery floor of the old cistern.

"One, two, three. Heave, boy," yelled Jim. "Don't let her stop."

With a sucking sound the cow move a step forward, then went to her nose. A neighbor on the rim of the caved in pit took up slack and pulled the cow's head up. Slowly they inched the reluctant animal up the ramp they had made of old lumber. Finally she stood on firm ground bellowing her disgust of the whole mess.

"I'll take her to the barn," said the neighbor. "You get started on the other one."

"Right-o," said Jim. "Buck up, Torv. We're half done."

Unable to answer for fear of getting a mouthful of muck, Torval slogged to the rear of the second trapped animal. The two cows had escaped from a pen in the early hours of the morning. Their jaunt ended when they fell through the roof of an old cistern. The shallow brick lined basin was half full of slush and debris and proved to be the perfect trap. By the time the neighbor tossed the rope halter down to them they had the cow at the ramp.

"This one's smaller. Must be a yearling," said Jim. He haltered the cow and handed the end of the lead rope up to the waiting crowd.

The cow was hauled out of the pit in short order and the growing crowd of by standers helped Jim and Torval up to safety. With much back slapping and a chorus of "atta boys" and "well dones" the conquering heroes were escorted home.

Ellen met them at the door and demanded they use the back entrance. They shucked vile boots and clothing on the stoop and trooped obediently to the tub of steaming water for a good wash.

"And you thought you were done with cows, Torv."

"Poor boy. Let me get this gunk out of your hair," said Ellen.

"Get his ears. No telling what's in there."

It wasn't until he was thoroughly clean that Torval felt it safe to open his mouth. He took a towel and muttered a thank you to Ellen.

"The boy can speak," said Jim.

"No thanks to you," said Ellen. "What were you thinking?"

"No thinking. Just brawn."

"On the farm we'd just shoot cows in trouble. Haul them out with a team and butcher them," said Torval. "Did you see old lady Marsden?"

"What is she up to now?"

"Used her good towels to wipe that cow dry. My ma never even let us use her good linen," said Torval. "For company she'd say."

"Was it her cow, then?" said Ellen.

"Naw. The old biddy's a bleedin' heart," said Jim. "Takes in stray dogs too."

~~~

Christmas arrived with its usual flurry of gift exchange and over eating. Klara's small charges alternated between wild with excitement and bouts of sulky tantrums. Lack of sleep, unusual hours for mealtime and bedtime added to the stress.

Never-the-less, time passed and the new year dawned clear and cold.

"Resolutions for the new year?" said Mr. Lawrence. "Anyone? Tillie?"

Tillie refilled the milk pitcher and brought more toast from the kitchen before she answered. "Find me a good husband and settle down."

"You said that last year," said Mrs. Lawrence. "What would we do without you."

"What about Jack?" said Klara.

"Jack? He's a boy. Good fun, but hardly a provider," said Tillie.

"But you like him." said Klara. "And he's good looking."

"Take a lesson from Tillie." said Mr. Lawrence. "Outward appearances can be deceiving."

"What about Klara's beau?" said Tillie. "Do you think he's a good catch?"

"Didn't know Klara had a beau."

"Who is he?"

"Jack's cousin." said Tillie. "Lives in Sioux Falls."

"He's not," said Klara. She busied herself buttering the children's toast and helping the youngest with his milk cup. She blushed to the tips of her ears.

"I see," said Mr. Lawrence. "Perhaps I should check up on this fellow."

Klara jerked her head up and one of the boys up-ended his cup at the same time. Milk spewed everywhere. She carried the child to the kitchen for a mop up. Tillie joined her to help.

"Sorry. I make big mess."

"Silly goose," said Tillie. "He's joshing you. Teasing."

"So complexilated," Klara gently wiped the child's face.

"Complicated? Where are you getting these high flying words?"

"Now we finish breakfast," said Klara. "No more flying milk."

~~~

1900 became 1901 with or without resolutions. Winter continued to grip the Dakotas; Torval rescued trapped cattle and learned the fine art of mixing cold elixir, while Klara helped the Lawrence boys along their journey to adulthood. Pork chops cost a dime a pound, sugar six cents. Bread was a nickel for a one pound loaf and a bushel of potatoes would set you back thirty-nine cents. The first great Texas oil gusher came in on January 10th and Queen Victoria died on January 22nd.

~~~

"Well the old Queen is dead," said Mr. Lawrence. "Now Edward has his chance."

"Weary with the waiting," said Mrs. Lawrence. "How old was Victoria?"

"It says she was 81. Died peacefully with her family around her."

Klara removed a pendant from around her neck. "The Queen."

"Ah, yes. An old shilling. That's the young queen bust."

"My friend gave it to me before I left home. For luck."

"And has it? Brought you luck?"

"I'm here," said Klara. "It was a little bumpy, but now smooth."

"Will they put Edward on the money now?"

"Probably minting the coins as we speak."

"School time," said Klara. "Come boys." She helped them fold their napkins beside their breakfast plates and push their chairs back under the table.

"I bet Klara's learning more than the boys," said Mrs. Lawrence.

"Best way to learn is to teach someone else."

~~~

While Klara was learning English and the manners of a middle class home, Torval struggled with the intricacies of Jim's collection of bottles, labels, mixing spoons and weighing scales. He poured over recipes for blending potions for man and beast. And the more he learned, the less he knew.

"It's no use, Jim." said Torval. "I'll never get it right."

"Nonsense, boy. It's a matter of patience and paying attention."

"What if I poison somebody?"

"Can't happen. This stuff is harmless. The powerful stuff is locked up."

"How can it help then? Why not buy from the traveling medicine shows?"

"Never know what you're getting there."

"Do you think they'll open the Rosebud to homesteaders?"

"Still hankering for the wide open spaces?"

"Will they?"

"No doubt. Just a matter of time."

"Has the railroad reached Montana yet?"

"God, Himself, hasn't reached Montana yet." Said Jim. "I hear that fellow with the talking horse is coming to town."

~~~

And neither had the Lindblads, Sophie and Arvid. Reached Montana, that is.

A BAD, BAD LAND

Thieves in the Night

~~~Sophia and Arvid~~~

The exhausted travelers had quickly descended into a deep sleep, all except Arvid. A thrill of excitement and a new plan surged through him. He slipped out to find the bell boy's hand cart. Quiet as a cat he moved their mostly packed baggage into the hallway, then trundled it to the lobby. He slipped back to be sure he had everything before he carried the sleeping baby to join the baggage. Little Lily he carried down next. When she awoke, he admonished her to look after her baby brother before he returned to the room.

"Sophie, wake up," said Arvid. "Quiet now. And hurry."

"What's wrong?"

"Nothing. Get dressed. Make any noise and I'll clock you good."

"The babies?"

"The kids are in the lobby waiting for us."

"My things?"

"All packed and waiting. Carry your shoes. I'll be along in a jiffy."

In the lobby Sophie found Lily sitting against the wainscoting, wide-eyed and drippy nosed, holding baby Matty. Arvid ran into the room.

"Hurry now. We need to catch the work train."

"Klara, what about Klara?"

"She'll be fine."

~~~

The work camp where Arvid had been hired on as second boss turned out to be a cluster of tents on the prairie near the town of

Evarts. The Chicago, Milwaukee and St. Paul Railroad had advanced far into Northwestern South Dakota and planned to arrive at its terminus before winter. Hopeful ranchers had constructed stock pens and sheds on the banks of the Missouri River and were busy funneling cattle to this shipping point for points east. The price of beef on the hoof was the highest ever seen and they all wanted a part of the pie, the money pie.

"Is this Montana?" said Sophie. "It's a dump."

"First we have to finish the track to Evarts," said Arvid. "See all that dust across the river? That's the stock yard. They're waiting for us."

"What about Montana? The little white house you promised."

"Wait long enough and this track will go clean to the Pacific Ocean," said Arvid. He pushed his way to the door of the rail car. "Hurry up. I want to inspect the work before dark." Arvid hastily helped Sophie and the babies down from the train before he disappeared into the crowd of workmen.

With the help of the railroad agent Sophie located the tent assigned to them and began the tedious process of setting up a household. Being the only woman in the camp brought forth a steady stream of helpers and gawkers. Her baggage and other possessions were piled next to the tent and a canvas shelter was procured to cover them from the weather.

"Now you can pick out what you need at your leisure, Missus."

"Your husband can find more permanent storage in the morning."

"Where is Arvid?" said Sophie. "Where do we get supplies? Food?"

"I expect you can eat with the crew. We done et already, but I'll send the cook over shortly."

~~~

Somehow Sophie and the babies survived those first weeks in the work camp while the railroad bridge was constructed. Arvid proved to be a forceful boss able to coerce his workers to great efforts. He set up a competition between the crews with a half day break, extra food and games as the prize. He even found a wagoneer willing and able to haul in several kegs of beer to oil his scheme.

The fall deadline for the rail link loomed, but so did the iron bridge. The day the first rail touched the opposite shore fireworks and hard liquor were provided by the waiting ranchers. The work camp moved across the river. The last rails with loading sidings and a temporary round house to turn the trains quickly sprouted from the barren ground. Within four years Evarts would become a major cattle shipping point.

"Time to move on, Sophie," said Arvid. "Time's a wasting."

"Montana?"

"A house anyway. Winter is blowin in before long."

"Thank God."

"They're building a spur line from Meckling west with grain collection points to help the farmers get their crops to eastern markets. Small potatoes, but it will get us through the winter. Then Montana."

So the Lindblads moved into a railroad house not thirty miles from where Klara was working.

Talking Horse, Silent Beau

~~~Klara and Torval~~~

The whole county was a buzz about the news. Jackson Von Schmidt and his phenomenal horse, Cotton King, had announced an appearance at the Sioux Falls fair grounds. Handbills and announcements soon plastered the county and beyond.

"Put these up around town, Torv," said Jim. He handed over a stack of advertising flyers offering free passes to the big show with a two dollar purchase.

"Admission is five cents?" said Torval. "I could buy a whole hatful of licorice whips for that. Do you think people will pay that to see a trained horse?"

"Back east they pay three times that much to see Beautiful Jim Key," said Jim.

"Who? Never heard of him."

"The super deluxe version of Cotton King. Does arithmetic, spells, reads minds. Tells the future."

"Trickery." said Torval. "Does Von Schmidt sell patent medicine?"

"No. I checked. Wouldn't want to support competition. He sells buttons, toys, pamphlets, souvenir stuff."

"Well, I might have to see for myself."

"Invite that girl of yours. I'll send Jack a couple of tickets. You can make a day of it."

~~~

"Does this horse really talk?" said Tillie. "I knew a lady had a talking bird."

"Naw. Horse just picks out cards with letters on them. Grabs them with his teeth and puts them on a board."

"Shoot. I wanted to hear him talk. Like them myna birds."

"Where do you want to sit," asked Jack. "Down front?"

"No," said Torval. "Not too close. We might want to skip out."

The foursome handed over their tickets and filed into the tent which smelled of fresh sawdust. A small band recruited locally entertained up front near the platform. Hawkers moved up and down the aisles selling postcards, buttons, and ribboned badges with Cotton King's picture. Others sold peanuts and root beer.

Once the crowd settled a man in a top hat walked to the front of the platform and called a woman from the audience. Clad in her Sunday best, Mrs. Marsden stepped up next to the announcer.

"What's she doing there?" said Torval. "The old bleeding heart."

"Hush," said Tillie. "Listen."

"…Miss Bessie Marsden from the local humane society," said the announcer. "She has a few words for us."

A few of the boys and young men stood up to whistle and jeer. Torval joined them until Klara pulled him back down. The announcer demanded silence.

"If any of you fine people would be willing to sign a pledge to always be kind to animals, I will have the cards at the end of the show." Bessie held the cards above her head, then made a hasty retreat to the rear of the tent.

"Thank you Miss Bessie," said the top-hatted man. "Now. Without further ado I give you Professor Jackson Von Schmidt and the phenomenal equine, Cotton King."

The curtain at the back of the tent parted to reveal a short gray-haired man with handlebar mustaches and glittery tuxedo. However, the crowd only had eyes for the lanky bay horse at his shoulder. The horse wore neither halter nor bridle, but walked freely into the tent. He paused when he came to Miss Bessie and bowed low so she could pat his velvet nose. She offered a pledge card which the bay horse took in his teeth. After a suitable pause he proceeded to the platform steps ignoring the outstretched hands of other audience members. At the steps he faced the crowd, then presented the card to one of the young rowdies standing nearby. The crowd roared.

With a knowing look, the horse stepped carefully onto the platform.

"Well, then, Cotton, can you greet the people?"

The horse looked at Von Schmidt, twitched his ears, canted his head.

"Come on, Cotton. These splendid folk have paid good money to see you."

The horse looked away.

"What's wrong with you?"

The horse ambled over to the stand which held a series of cards with letters and numbers. He plucked out a 'C' and put it on the display stand. An 'O' followed by a 'T' came next until he had spelled out 'COTTON KING.'

"Are you saying you must be properly addressed?"

The horse nodded and the crowd murmured.

"Good people, may I present Cotton King, smartest horse in the west. Now, where are we, Cotton? What is the name of this burg?"

The band produced a drum roll. Cotton pricked up his ears and swaggered to the front of the stage to bow to the crowd. They answered with clapping and cheers.

The horse then plucked a card from the stand and placed it on the rack facing the crowd. The crowd groaned when they saw a 'T' card. Cotton ignored them and fetched an 'A,' then an 'O.' He paused before he produced a 'C' and placed it at the front of his row of letters. He bowed several times to the cheering crowd before adding the two 'N' cards.

With the tone set, the hero and the villain clearly marked, the show began. Cotton answered questions with the cards or by nodding 'yes' and 'no.' He reprimanded Von Schmidt by turning his backside to the little professor when he made mistakes.

The two played the shell game on a table tilted to allow the audience full view of the action. Von Schmidt moved the oversized shells in intricate patterns to confound his opponent and the horse picked the wrong shell more times than not. Finally, in mock glee, the professor brought out a wad of bills and waved them under the horse's nose.

"Let's make this interesting," he said. "My week's salary. What do you have?"

With a snort Cotton King trotted to the back of the stage where a suitcase sat. He nosed it open and removed a parcel wrapped in brown paper. He carried it back and dropped it at Von Schmidt's feet.

Von Schmidt unwrapped a large silver cup and held it over his head for the audience to see.

"Your Kentucky Fair world champion cup? You want to put your cup against my money? You'll lose, you know."

Cotton nodded yes.

"Candy from a baby."

Cotton nosed the correct shell first try and Von Schmidt demanded best two out of three. The horse snorted and pulled back his lips, but nodded his yes. He picked the right shell again and grabbed it in his teeth. He waved it at the audience, then pranced around the stage with the little professor at his heels.

"Cheat. You cheated," roared the little man. To the audience he said, "You saw that? He cheated. Right?"

The audience roared back their disagreement. Cotton bowed and tossed the shell into the crowd. One of the rowdies retrieved it. Cotton took the shell in his teeth, bowed and turned to Von Schmidt.

"You want your money. You. You ungrateful wretch." He placed the roll of bills in the trophy. "Anyone want to try your luck against the horse?"

Cotton turned to the audience and pointed to an eager fellow seated midway up the aisle.

Von Schmidt hauled him up on stage and explained the procedure.

"I will move the shells and you two predict the outcome. Of course we need another shell. Two players, four shells. Bill here will hold the stakes." He motioned to a helper who had appeared from backstage.

Back in the audience, Klara felt a growing anxiety. "Tillie, I know that one."

"What are you talking about?"

"Something wrong?" said Torval. "Tell me, Klara."

"It's Arvid. My friend Sophia's husband. Is he with a woman?"

"Not that I can see. Looks like a group of railroad workers."

As the game progressed on stage with the horse winning more and more of Arvid's money, Klara related the story of her abandonment and her stolen money.

"By gor, I'd like to tear him limb from limb," said Torval.

"I think he's getting his just desserts," said Jack. "Best not to meddle or we'll all end up in the pokey."

"What a fool. To think he could win against that pair."

"Why is that?" asked Klara. "Why can't he win? Arvid always wins."

"You think that horse is picking the shell. The professor there is telling the horse which one."

"I can't see the signals," said Tillie. "He doesn't touch the horse."

"Me either. He's good, believe me."

"It's a set up, a fool's game," said Jack. "Me thinks we should slip out now."

"We haven't seen the grand finale," said Tillie.

"There won't be a finale if the sheriff gets wind of this gambling," said Jack.

The foursome slipped out the back exit and hurried to their buggy.

"Maybe we should wait. Clobber that Arvid guy when he comes out," said Torval.

"Believe me, he's getting clobbered as we speak. He won't have a thin dime when the professor gets done with him," said Jack. "I've seen this before."

"Jack's right," said Klara. "I hope Sophia is all right."

"How can anyone be all right married to that jerk."

"They must be living around here somewhere."

"I thought you said they were going to Montana." said Tillie.

"Ah. Montana," said Torval. "Don't you wish you could go homesteading?"

"Hard work."

"Freedom."

Still chattering about the pros and cons of free land, Jack clucked the horses into a trot and headed back to town.

Free Land is Seldom Free

~~~Sophia~~~

Arvid and Sophie shuffled from job to job dragging their children and goods behind them. Then, Arvid got word that the government had opened more reservation land to homesteaders.

"Get to packing, girl."

"Montana?"

"Not quite."

"We're doing good here, Arvid," said Sophie. "You got a good job, we have this little house."

"It ain't ours, woman." Arvid paced back and forth nearly engulfing the tiny kitchen. "Free land. Think about that."

Instead Sophie thought about the girl she had found to help with the children and housework. Strange girl that Talusa. "Can Talusa come with us?"

"Are you daft?"

Sophie would have many occasions to remember her hired maid over the next few years. She had learned many things from her. At the weekly ironings sessions Sophie kept the fire up and carried the hot irons, while Talusa muscled the flat irons through mountains of wrinkles and talked. Tales of swamp creatures, hauntings, miraculous cures, potions and remedies for all manner of problem. Unknown to Arvid, the two women often did laundry for neighbors to earn spending money. Sophie would lose both her helper and her source of cash.

"Please, Arvid."

"Start packing." He headed for the door. "No more nonsense about dragging that biddy with us."

So Sophie prepared to give up the railroad house, while Arvid talked endlessly.

"Free land."

"Says who?"

"Can't pass it up. We'll be rich."

Free, my stars and garters. Toil and trouble beyond imagining. No chained slave would put up with this life, thought Sophie. When I married Arvid, back in the old country, we planned to live with his parents and help work the family farm. My family was dead and gone and Arvid was loving and attentive. As that year wore on I realized I was little more than an unpaid servant and the work load could do nothing but grow. I was so happy when Arvid decided to emigrate.

Arvid had all manner of wild ideas. He brought home numerous money making schemes. Everything from selling tonic door-to-door, to going to Australia as sheep ranchers. The trouble with all of his ideas was money or, rather, the lack of it. His father told him he could expect no help from him. The farm was good enough for him and his grandparents before him, it should be good enough for us.

They had managed to acquire only a few kronur, when some distant cousins came through on their way to the emigrant ships in Gothenburg. They had maps, pamphlets, and new dreams. Arvid asked them a hundred questions, but hardly sat still long enough to hear the answers when he learned a person could earn free passage by signing up a group paying emigrants. Arvid was a good talker, a smooth back slapper. It was the perfect solution.

The idea of free land, a place of their own, was like a song in the morning. Sophie caught herself smiling at odd moments, flicking dish suds at Arvid when he walked through the kitchen, and dancing with her apron at the clothesline. Arvid's mother was sure her daughter-in-law was possessed by the devil.

After they abandoned Klara, they traveled across South Dakota in a work train, a common freight car jammed with tools and supplies. They had left Canton in the middle of the night with only their hand baggage and the children. Arvid promised the railroad would ship their belongings on the first freight. What he failed to mention was that they had to build the permanent tracks and station first.

This time the Lindblads traveled to the Redbud claim on an immigrant train. Box cars filled with hopeful families and all their worldly goods. By the time they reached Murdo Sophie half expected to be left behind. Arvid had spent the last hour holding her while she puked out the open door of the box car. She felt sorry for him, but in the long run it was his own fault. Weak with relief, she jumped out when the train stopped a short distance from the Murdo station to await shuttling onto a siding. They had been on the move for some twelve hours.

After a break to tend the livestock the journey continued. It became even rougher and Sophie declined breakfast. The children seemed unfazed and slept most of the way. Perhaps the sips of whiskey Arvid plied them with had much to do with that.

While Sophie dozed, he started a poker game with some of the other travelers. He managed to win eighteen dollars before he passed out. His new friends dragged him to the back of the rail car and left him snoring where Sophie found him the next morning. She helped herself to a share of his winnings. Hard earned money, she thought.

The settlers unloaded in the middle of no where. Without the benefit of the regular ramps and chutes of a rail yard, unloading heavy goods and livestock was difficult. But working in concert with each other and railroad employees anxious to move on, they managed to unload everything.

"We have to have the rocking chair," said Sophie. "For nursing the baby."

"Baby? Not another squalling brat. How did you let that happen?"

"I'm sorry, Arvid. Please load the rocking chair."

"It will not fit, woman." said Arvid. "Who takes furniture to the prairie."

"If we had bought a freight wagon like I wanted…"

"Shut up about that damn wagon. This high top buggy is the latest model."

"At least load the house plunder so I can cook a proper meal."

They arranged and rearranged things, but it was clear that things had to be left behind. The rocking chair and the box of house plunder were the first items abandoned along the tracks.

Sophie shouted, "Leave the firewood. And the glass windows."

"We need them for the new house."

"The weather won't hurt them. We can drive back for them later."

In the end the battle was a vain one. They left rocking chair, most of the firewood, windows, the sheet iron stove, and the heavier tools.

Sophie tried hard not to cry as they drove off, but even Arvid noticed and offered his handkerchief. He said not to worry, he'd drive back in the morning to get the rest of their things. He could be awfully sweet at times, thought Sophie.

They made quite a cavalcade winding through the huge piles of Russian thistle searching out a reasonably level path to the home sites. The McClearys, the family the Lindblads were to travel with on the first part of the overland trek, led the way. They had a cutter and a freight wagon, both loaded to capacity with chairs, lumber, tools, and children. Two milk cows, three riding horses, and a number of goats were tied behind. Crates of chickens, ducks, and even a few turkeys were lashed in back of the house goods. A small organ with its carved stool had been lovingly stowed just behind the driver's seat in the big wagon. Sophie knew the barrels and boxes held linens and china because Mrs. McCleary had told her all about each item. She said they had homesteaded before, before the six children had been born, and she had been so terribly unhappy in the bare cabin built by her husband and brother. She vowed she would never again be without her precious things, so when her husband decided to move farther west, she insisted on bringing all her pretties, pretties that had been in storage at her sister's house in Mason City all these years.

Sophie envied her fine belongings, but they certainly slowed progress. Each hill, each dry wash, had to be inspected to see if the heavy wagon could safely cross without undue bumping. Several times fragile items had to be unloaded and hand carried over a particularly rough place. It was with regret, but also with relief that the two families finally parted company a few hours later.

"Sure glad to be shut of those McClearys," said Arvid.

"I thought she was nice," said Sophie. "And she entertained the children."

"Bragging about all their fine stuff."

"It was nice to talk about fashions and art and society."

"Don't be getting high falutin notions, wanting things and all."

"Sorry, Arvid."

The silence of the prairie closed around them. Even Arvid felt it. He started singing all the silly songs they had learned as children and effectively stonewalled further talk.

When they reached Peach Creek, the singing stopped. A steep bank barred their way.

"Where are we?" said Sophie. "Hush, Lily. Come walk with me." She lifted the little girl from her perch on the buggy seat.

"We must have missed the ford," said Arvid. "You let those kids distract me. All that whining and crying."

"Are we above or below the ford?"

"No idea."

"The children are tired and hungry. Me too."

"Hush, woman. Let me think."

They decided to cross where they were. The near bank was steep and muddy from the spring rains. The horse was tired, not used to pulling the heavy buggy over such rough ground. He balked when urged to move forward, so everyone climbed out and Arvid tried to lead the beast down the bank. When that failed, Arvid hit him a couple of hard licks with the whip, but the horse threw up his head and planted his hooves more firmly.

"Stop, Arvid," said Sophie. "Unhitch and lead him across."

"Shut up, woman." He hit the horse across the face with the butt of the whip.

"You're hurting him."

"I'll show you hurt if you don't get out of my way."

Sophie held her ground and in the end they unhitched the poor animal and led him across the creek. The sobbing children watched from the buggy.

By the time they reached the far bank they were weighted down with sticky mud. They scraped off as much of the mud as they could, then tied the horse to a low hanging branch to wait, while Arvid and Sophie crossed back to unload the buggy and carry the stuff across. Only Arvid's yellow pup was happy, racing back and forth across the mud, leaping into the water to swim, then shake.

Hours later Arvid had Lily climb on his back, while he carried

Matty across the muddy creek. The buggy itself was another matter. Arvid finally shucked off his mud-stiff pants and rode the horse back across the creek, hitched him to the empty buggy, and rode back, buggy lurching behind. The cow tethered behind complained loudly, but followed willingly.

It was a sorry group that staggered onto the new homestead. The mess and worry of fording Peach Creek dimmed in the disappointment of that first impression of their new home. They had bought an existing claim instead of starting from scratch. Arvid had inspected it a few months ago, before the fierce spring rains. The corners were marked with rock piles and the outlines of a small sod building poked up through the grass. Lacking a roof, the walls had eroded away in the rain.

"Where's the tar paper shack?" said Sophie. "You promised." No trace of it was visible.

"Must have been scavenged for material." Arvid stood shaking his head. "Damn settlers. Damn Indians. Damn everybody to hell."

Sophie stared at her new home. "Maybe it will look better in daylight."

"Ha. Little Miss Sunbeam. If it hadn't taken you so long to pack," said Arvid.

"Blame later. Right now the problem is supper and a place to sleep."

While Arvid unhitched, Sophie found the crude remains of a fire pit, cleared away the dry weeds, and started water to heating. She had salvaged the enamel coffee pot and iron skillet from the box of house goods left on the siding, so she had coffee ready for Arvid when he finished scraping mud clods from the animals and himself.

"Just bread and jam for supper."

"It's good, Pappa," said Lily. She had her mouth crammed full.

"Damn pap," said Arvid. He wolfed down several slices.

"Watch your language, Arvid. The children."

"More," said Lily. "Matty, too."

Washing up would have to wait until daylight because they had used all the water they had carried from the creek. Arvid promised he would haul water from Wall when he went back for the goods left behind. Wall was the nearest town, though Arvid was unsure of the distance because he had not been there before.

It was full dark by the time the weary travelers were ready to sleep. Arvid said it was no use to light the oil lamp, so they fumbled around in the dark until they found a smooth place to sleep. Sophie shucked off her muddy skirt and shoes and rolled herself in a quilt with the children.

When they awoke just before dawn, a thin crust of frost covered everything. Frost in June, they should have known it was a portent of trouble. Sophie pulled the quilt over her head and held the babies close.

"Get up, Soph," said Arvid. "Need my breakfast."

"Go away."

"Up, Up. Greet the dawn."

"It's still dark."

"Wrong," said Arvid. He grabbed the edge of the quilt and jerked.

The first light dribbled over the horizon as Arvid wrapped himself in the still warm quilts and sat down against the buggy wheel. He wanted his coffee and a hot breakfast.

Sophie was shaking with cold by the time she got back to camp with an armload of sticks. By the time Arvid finished his coffee and bread he was bubbling with plans to drive to Wall.

"First I'll buy a water tank, arrange to have it brought out."

"Food, we need milk and flour. Bacon."

"I can detour to the siding and pick up our stuff on the way back."

"Help me make a list."

So while Sophie dictated, Arvid wrote out a list with a stub pencil on an old envelope. She complained that she didn't know what was available or how much it cost, but finally settled for staples like coffee, bread, sugar, and soap. Arvid hitched up the horse and drove off through the wasteland in the general direction they had come the day before. He said he could find the ford from this side and he should be back by supper time.

The morning went quickly. In anticipation of Arvid's return Sophie unpacked and set up camp as best she could. She hung the quilts over a scrub oak to air, worked the drying mud from her skirt, tried to clean her shoes, scoured the frying pan. All while trying to soothe and entertain the children.

By noon she knew she had to water the animals. She was afraid to release the chickens from their crate so she took the coffee pot and walked the mile or so back to Peach Creek for water.

The yellow pup followed her, sometimes bumping against her legs, never ranging out of sight. The dry bread he had for breakfast didn't agree with him and he gagged and hacked up every few steps. At the creek he rolled in the mud and lapped up a stomach full of water, most of which he threw up on the way back to camp. Sophie poured water into the fry pan and let the chickens out of the crate to drink and forage for bugs. The pup made a dive for the chickens and upset the water pan.

"Lily, tie up the pup," said Sophie. "I'm taking the cow to the creek for a drink."

While the cow drank, Sophie tried to wash the mud from her skirt and shoes, then filled the coffee pot again. The mud, both dry and fresh, stuck like cement. She finally gave up and led the cow back to camp. For once she was glad to be alone because she wore only her chemise and petticoat.

She turned the cow loose to scrounge what little grass she could find and hung her ruined clothes on a bush. The shoes she rubbed with a bacon end.

Arvid had spent an unreasonable chunk of money on work clothes before they left Sioux Falls. Now Sophie decided to try a pair of his overalls. Before the hour was out it was as if she had never worn anything else. With the money she had squirreled away in her sewing box she vowed to buy a pair of work boots at the next opportunity.

That resolve lifted her spirits and she spent the rest of the afternoon making the camp snug and comfortable. Though the coffee water was hot and the beans and bacon cooked, Arvid did not show up for supper. Just after sunset she gave up, threw the ruined beans to the yellow pup, and crawled into her nest of quilts with the children. She jerked awake at each new sound in the night, but none of them announced Arvid's arrival. Just before dawn she fell into a deep sleep and did not stir until the cow's low moans penetrated her brain.

Sophie finally realized the cow must be in trouble. Groggy, almost drunk with sleep, she tried to pull on her stiff shoes.

"Mommy, mommy," cried Lily. "I'm hungry."

"In a minute, Baby," Said Sophie. Her head ached, her mouth tasted bitter as a copper spoon, her stomach lurched. She gave up and hurled her shoes at the yellow pup who was growling and dragging the quilts through the dirt.

The dog knocked over the water she had carried in for morning washing and coffee. Lily and Matty's complaints turned to howls of outrage. Sophie wanted to sit on the ground and join them, but finally hustled herself barefoot through the brush to the cow.

The poor beast was standing at the bottom of a dry wash, her hind end wet with birthing water, the tiny hooves of her calf barely visible. All business now, Sophie checked to be sure it was the front hooves and that they were pointing the right way indicating a normal delivery. She quickly saw the real reason for the cow's anxiety. A half dozen coyotes appeared like silent shadows against the opposite side of the gully. They were prepared to sit and wait.

Sophie's exhaustion was bone deep, her rage white hot as she drove the predators away from the helpless cow again and again. Their attack grew fiercer when the calf finally slipped from the birth canal and the cow turned to clean her newborn.

The cow suddenly decided Sophie was one of the predators and charged her when she got too close. That left her calf open to attack by the coyotes. They were all frantic by the time Arvid's voice joined the screams of the children on the bank above.

"Down here," shouted Sophie. "Bring your rifle."

"Damn, woman. Can't leave you for a minute."

"Shoot them."

Double quick Arvid had the coyotes on the run and the cow and calf back to the relative safety of the camp.

Sophie had hoped to hear a few words of praise for her efforts. Instead Arvid told her how silly she was to be afraid of a few mangy coyotes; laughed at her worry over his absence; jeered the sight of her in his overalls. She consoled herself with the knowledge that the cow had birthed a healthy bull calf and they would have a supply of fresh milk in a few days.

Silver Needles, Silver Dragons

~~~Klara~~~

At breakfast Klara and Tillie were grilled about the talking horse. Even the sleepy-eyed boys listened to their story of the beautiful Cotton King.

"He could count. And spell words," said Klara.

"Nah. Horses can't spell," said the older boy.

"Better than Klara," said Tillie. "A real looker, too"

"Perhaps we should have taken the boys," said Mrs. Lawrence.

Tillie nodded disapproval and whispered about the gambling in her ear.

"Oh. Well. A good thing they are on their way to Kansas City, then."

"Perhaps a real circus will come to town this summer," said Mr. Lawrence.

"Can we go, Papa? Please, Papa?"

"What is circus?" said Klara.

Everyone started explaining about clowns, elephants, tigers, and trapeze flyers until Klara's head felt like it was bursting with new words. "Stop, stop. I am confronted."

"Confused?' said Tillie.

"Confounded?" said Mr. Lawrence. "What are you teaching this girl, Tillie?"

"Maybe it's time she had proper instruction in English," said Mrs. Lawrence.

"Oh no. Please. I will try harder," said Klara.

"Why not take her to your sewing circle. The chit chat would be good for her. The boys can do without her for a few hours a week."

"Not a bad idea. We're starting a new project."

~~~

Klara followed her employer into the Canton Community Hall with the sewing basket. She hesitated in the hallway.

"Come on, Klara," said Mrs. Lawrence. "They are nice ladies. They don't bite."

"Maybe the boys are needing something. I could run check."

"Tillie is quite capable of holding down the fort."

"Fort? What is fort?"

"Never mind. Bring the basket."

The group of women and girls seated around the room greeted them effusively. Piles of bright scraps were laid out on two long tables. Colored thread, beads and sequins, tiny pins, patterns, squares of black velvet, squares of cardboard, and waxed paper.

They found a place and produced scissors and needles from the basket. Klara suffered through introductions and words of encouragement, but was spared further misery by the entrance of the teacher. The prim, quick handed woman got down to business by introducing herself as Miss Kaylon Birdie. "I'm from Maryland. Visiting my sister-in-law." She indicated a dark-haired lady sitting near the demonstration table. "She thought I should share this art form with you all."

Her audience of about twenty ladies chorused a greeting, then waited expectantly.

"This is called Victorian Couch art. It has been very popular in Europe." She held up several framed pictures of elaborate flowers and a larger scene with a horse and carriage crossing a bridge. They were worked with metallic thread on black velvet. Many of the details were done with beads and tiny sequins. A puffed effect added to the three dimensional look of the horse and the flowers.

"Oh. Very pretty."

"Is it hard to do? It looks difficult."

"Here are the patterns. Pick out what you like."

Everyone gathered around the table to examine the choices. Most popular was a simple lily design. Klara favored the scenic pictures until she spied one with a bold silver horse.

"This one," she said. "Saint Jorge and the evil dragon. I know this story."

"Are you sure? It's not very pretty."

"Absolute sure." Klara ran her fingers over the lines of the horse and rider. "My brother painted big dragon on our wall at home."

"He painted on the wall?"

"Many homes have painted walls," said Klara. She went on to explain about a retired soldier who embellished walls, beams, buckets and utensils with flowers, leaves, and looping whorls in return for board and room. "He would stay a few days, then move on."

"So why did your brother paint your wall?"

"He saw the dragon at church. I gave him paint for present."

Klara was saved further explanation by the teacher calling her pupils to order. She demonstrated laying out the pattern with chalk and stretching the velvet over an embroidery frame. Only the most experienced ladies were ready to thread their needles at the end of class. Klara's work was a bit smudgy, but she did have the entire pattern laid out on her velvet.

"Good, girl," said Miss Birdie. "I have some sequins that might suit that design perfectly. I'll bring them next time."

Angel Sequins for Saint George

Retail Reverses

When is a Dollar not a Dollar

~~~Torval~~~

In May the railroad barons brought their battle to a grim climax. The stock market collapsed from the weight of their finagling. Investors far removed from rolling stock and steel rails lost their fortunes. Even the small town businessman trying to grow his profits buying supposedly safe stocks saw their efforts blowing in the wind.

His investments wiped out, Jim was unable to buy goods on credit. The store no longer offered the customer a plethora of choices. The shelf stock dwindled daily. He had Torval constantly rearranging jars, bottles, and boxes to make the store enticing to shoppers. He found odd bits of merchandise in the storeroom to add to the shelves. Last year's winter and Christmas items appeared at close-out prices. He mixed the contents of broken boxes of chocolates and mints in large jars to be sold by the piece.

"How is it going, Jim?" said Ellen. She examined her husband's efforts.

"Still looks pretty bare in here," he said. "I think I'll move the pharmacy up by the cash register."

"How about I move the hat making things over from the house," said Ellen. "Provide a little color."

"You could set up by the front window."

"Then rent out that extra room."

"I wouldn't hunt up a boarder just yet."

"Oh?" Ellen looked at Jim. "Something you're not telling me?"

"Jack may be coming home for awhile."

"I'll be glad to see him. Is he in some trouble again?"

"No, no. Just a casualty of hard times. Rumor is the Hansons are selling out."

"I'm sorry to hear that."

"Don't mention it just yet. I may be wrong."

"All right."

"How is the hat business these days?"

"Ladies are still buying," said Ellen. "A new hat peps up last year's dress."

That week Ellen brought her hat making materials to the store. The bundles of feathers and yards of fine velvet, net, and satin provided a colorful diversion for shoppers. She had Torval arrange a comfy chair and work table by the large window and she was soon spending hours there beading designs on velvet and satin, molding hat rims, and fitting her customers.

"So interesting to watch my hat in the making," said Mrs. Beards. "Like a Paris boutique."

"Would you like an extra plume on this band?"

"Yes, please," said Mrs. Beards. "You should have a few small tables. Serve coffee and pastries in the afternoon."

"That's a wonderful Idea."

"My niece has the knack for pastry making. She could use the work."

"I doubt we could pay her."

"She could work for commission and tips. Wouldn't put you out a cent."

With Torval's help the hat shop blossomed into a small cafe. He painted the drab walls, built a partition, and moved chairs from storage. Several of Ellen's friends sewed table covers for the wire spools Jim salvaged from the city dump. In a weekend the unused corner of the general store became El's Tea Room.

~~~

Torval and Jim stood in the middle aisle of the store. A new shipment of soaps and ointments, unloaded from the freight wagon, sat in a heap in front of them.

"This is not good, boy," said Jim. He read wholesale prices from the bill of lading. "We sold most of this stuff for less than we're being charged now."

"We have to raise our prices?"

"More than double. Double trouble."

"How can the customers afford a bar of soap at twice the price?"

"That's the rub, Torv." He ran his fingers through his hair and sat down on an up turned barrel. "The country's going to the dogs."

"What makes the prices go up?"

"Politicians, poor crops, too much debt. Who knows. Poor folks want higher wages. Rich folks get richer."

"I don't understand."

"Join the crowd. Maybe it has something to do with the railroads."

"How can railroads make the price of soap go up?"

"A couple of rail barons are fighting to control all the rail lines."

"All of them?"

"Well, maybe not all. Mostly the Great Northern."

"And if one person has control, he can charge as much as he wants."

"Looks that way."

"Higher freight costs mean higher prices."

"Better get cracking on those new price signs," said Jim. "Then you can start deliveries."

~~~

As Torval pedaled up Willow Street for his first delivery, he wondered about his father. Had this economic mess, dry conditions, and higher prices touched the farmer. A spark of guilt ignited. He had not been home for months. A visit was in order.

~~~

Torval wheeled his bike off the station platform. At the first crossroads he stopped to survey the patchwork of farm fields spread out before him. The wheat and corn seemed short for this time of year. The corn rattled in the wind and a fine haze of dust spread over Grand Valley. By the time he had pedaled the twenty minutes home he knew dust wasn't the only thing on the wind. Trouble hovered there, too.

When he wheeled into the farm yard, he could see that the usually pristine house was in need of paint, the barn door crashed in the wind, piles of trash littered the yard, and the windmill creaked with every turn.

Jack greeted him and they walked the bike to lean it against the garden fence.

"Your pop is in the barn."

Torval looked over the fence at the straggling rows of beans and hills of squash and cucumber. "Not a very good year is it?"

"Dry is what it is."

Torval found his father mending harness. How small he looks, thought Torval. Like a woolen sock in hot water, he thought. Except his beard which curled down over the bib of his overalls. After a curt, almost formal greeting the old man embraced his son.

"Good to see you," he said. "Let's see if your sister will put the kettle on."

They walked to the house with Jack tagging along behind. Carrie waited for them on the porch her apron flapping in the wind.

"Not a good day for biking is it, Torv." She led the way to the kitchen where both the tea kettle and the coffee pot hummed on the stove. "You'll really have a head wind on your way back."

"The whole valley looks dry," said Torval. "How is Mother?"

"Cups and cookies in a sec," said Carrie. She disappeared into the pantry.

Torval, Jack, and the old man settled themselves at the table. They scraped their chairs around, arranged the cups and spoons Carrie placed on the table, handed cookies around, fiddled with their coffee, stirred and sipped, and muttered about the weather. Torval stared out the window and wondered why he had come. Jack and the old man stared at the wall, the stove, the calendar on the wall, anything to avoid talking.

Finally, Carrie burst out, "Tell him, Father. For God's sake."

110

"Your mother's not doing so well. We're thinking about moving to town."

"And?"

"The bank is about to take the place."

"Unless we can sell first," said Carrie. "There are two brothers, new immigrants anxious to buy."

With Carrie and Jack's prompting, his father told him about a string of reversals. Bad weather, poor crops, a disease affecting the cattle limiting the spring calf crop, a second mortgage.

Torval's second cookie was dry in his mouth, dry as the blowing dust outside. Much of this had been happening while he still lived at home, yet he had not noticed. He barely heard Carrie explain that they had found a suitable house in town and that selling to the Arndt brothers would save the trouble of an auction. She would live with her parents for the time being to act as housekeeper and cook.

"What about Jack?" Torval finally got his mouth in gear. "Things aren't much better in Sioux Falls."

"I'll think of something," said Jack. "Maybe it's time to head west."

"Homestead?" Torval felt a stab of excitement. "A perfect solution for us."

"Maybe I could join you. Later. After the folks are settled," said Carrie.

"It would be a great adventure," said Jack. He looked at Torval. "I know, I know. I said I'd never do something like this, but I've changed my mind."

"Beats clerking in a shop or squinting over columns of figures," said Torval.

"Fellow has to eat and have some fun."

"What he really means is his girl dumped him," said Carrie.

"That Tillie?" said Torval. "I thought you two were tight."

"Said I'd never make anything of myself."

"Maybe she'll change her mind for a chance at homesteading."

~~~

Torval returned to the Canton station in time to catch the evening train into Sioux Falls. Jim and Ellen seemed almost relieved when he told them the plan he and Jack had hatched. Jim offered to look into the legal details when he tended to some business at the court house on Monday morning and Ellen wrote a short note of approval to Jack. In Torval's mind that left only the problem of Klara.

Aloud, he wondered if she would join their adventure.

"You could ask her," said Ellen. "Are you serious about this girl?"

"Marry her," said Jim. "You can't be traipsing around the prairie with a single lady."

"She can take out homestead papers, too. Give you twice as much land."

More than two hundred acres of land, thought Torval. A wife. What am I getting into. Aloud he said, "I should help my folks move first."

"Jack can help, too."

"You have a second cousin up state. Name of Erik Tolovson. He's been homesteading once before. I hear he wants to try again. Add a bit of experience to your expedition."

"I hate to leave you in the lurch. You've been good to me," said Torval.

"This was going to be your last payday anyway," said Jim. "The well is dry."

"Then, maybe, it's best for everyone."

Sod Cutting and Rug Cutting

~~~Sophia~~~

Thoughts of fresh milk for the children had made Sophie forget for a moment the precious rocking chair on the railroad siding miles away. Once the cow was squared away though, she checked through the pile of goods in the buggy.

"You didn't bring it?" said Sophie.

"Bring what? said Arvid. He was unloading sacks of flour and oats. "Got a good deal on the oats. Figure they will feed all the stock."

"The rocking chair."

"Oh. The water barrel took up a lot room." Of course he had forgotten it. By the time he finally hauled it home the sun had blistered and whitened its fine rubbed finish, loosened a spindle in the arm.

"What did you accomplish? You were gone for days."

"New shoes." Arvid held up a pair of shiny wing tips.

"Are you insane," said Sophie. "Do you have time to go dancing? You have children to feed, a house to build."

"Don't be a spoil sport, Soph. A man's got to have a little fun."

"Did you get bacon? How about the yeast? The sugar?"

"Umm. Yeast is in there somewhere. Couldn't afford the bacon."

"Afford? Afford? You had all the cash from your last two months on the railroad."

"I got in a little game. Lost a bit."

Speechless, Sophie stared at her husband. Resentment burned a hole deep into her heart.

"Buck up, Soph. We'll start cutting sod tomorrow. Have you snug as a bug in no time."

~~~

Rubbing her swollen hands, Sophie straightened up. Arvid was muttering something about supper. She thought about the long day of cutting sod for their house. She had worked alongside Arvid, matching him block on block, wrestling the fifty pound squares of earth and prairie roots to form the walls of the building.

"Supper? You want supper?"

"Get a fire going, Soph. Pancakes would be good."

It was nearly sundown. Sophie stopped work and went to gather dry grass and buffalo chips for the fire, while Arvid cut a few more blocks.

She had argued for a cold supper, but Arvid had to have his coffee and it seemed a shame to waste the fire. They had brought bundles of fire wood along on the immigrant train, but it was a precious commodity. Sophie worked hard to stretch it, make it last. She told herself she would carry a basket everywhere to collect bits of dry grass, greasewood, Russian thistle, anything that might burn. Even when she trekked up the gulch for necessary business.

Arvid slipped off to the creek to wash up and have a swim. He joined Sophie and the children when the smell of cooking filled the air.

"Too bad we don't have bacon," he said.

"Whose fault is that?"

"Bacon, bacon," chanted the children. "We like bacon."

"Don't talk with your mouth full," said Sophie. To Arvid she said, "You could hunt us some rabbit. There are hundreds of them out there."

Gathering cow chips for fuel

"Maybe, tomorrow," said Arvid, his mouth full of jam and pancake.

~~~

That tomorrow would never arrive, so Sophie took to carrying the rifle when she hunted firewood. Soon fried rabbit joined the beans or pancakes on the menu.

Her saving ways all came to naught the day some of Arvid's old cronies arrived on their way to a new claim over on Cedar creek.

"Guys. How are you? How's railroading?" said Arvid. "Stop and rest a bit."

"On our way to claims over near Spit Mountain," said Bill, the tall one.

"Sophie, this here's Bill. The red-head is Wayne. And here's Ellis."

"Pleased to meet you, Ma'am," they chorused.

Sophie was glad for the respite and hurried to make coffee. Arvid helped his friends unsaddle the horses and stake them out to graze the sparse grass. Bill produced a flask of whiskey from his saddle bags and spiked the coffee. The stories began.

Old tales, repetitions of shared experience, and a general catching up on the news spun on for hours. The men sat around the fire, talking and drinking whisky. Much to Sophie's horror, Arvid tossed more wood on the fire whenever it died down. She finally crawled into her roll of blankets and cried herself to sleep.

~~~

"You used all the wood." accused Sophie.

"I cut it. I'll burn it if I feel like it," said Arvid.

Sophie stormed off to take care of chores. Things looked brighter with her head pressed against the cow's soft flank. Streams of warm milk bounding off the sides of the pail. She always thought a fresh milk cow was better than a bar of gold.

She consoled herself with the good supply of fresh butter and soft cheese. She could feed her children. The clabbered milk fed the chickens and the yellow pup.

~~~

"Can we get some piglets to fatten?" said Sophie. "I hate wasting milk."

"I'll make a pen next to the cow's lean-to," said Arvid. "I need nails."

"Can't you use up the ones you bought for the roofing?"

"Too short. I need long ones."

"Another excuse to go to town. I'm coming along this time."

"Maybe we should wait for warmer weather."

"We're almost out of water, too."

Water continued to be a big problem. Washing up and water for the animals was hauled from Peach Creek, but Arvid hauled water by the barrel from Wall for the household use. A barrel of water lasted less than a week in the dry season. Arvid enjoyed his trips to town and Sophie always thought that was the reason he never made much progress developing a better water system.

Most of that first summer was consumed with cutting sod for the house and hauling water. Between bouts of morning sickness Sophie planted a scrap of garden, but blistering heat and lack of water soon withered the tender plants. She didn't get to town with Arvid until the first hard frost.

"We need tar paper for the roof," said Arvid one frosty morning.

"Supplies for winter, too," said Sophie. "I need shoes."

She had gone barefoot all summer and needed shoes in the worst way. At first Arvid was reluctant to let her come with him. He insisted he could get the right size shoes, but Sophie held out and in the end made her first trip to Wall.

Wall was a welcome, almost overwhelming experience. Sophie had not spoken to a single soul, other than Arvid and the children, for months. After they bought flour, sugar, coffee, corn meal, salt, a side of bacon, roofing nails, long nails, and tar paper, she left Arvid to entertain himself at the saloon.

With Lily and Matty clinging to her skirt Sophie returned to the general store. She bought work boots, lard oil, a red checked oil cloth for the table, and a new mixing bowl.

"My husband ruined my bowl. He used it to stir up some gooey concoction for the horse's hooves."

"No hoof, no horse," said the clerk. "What else?"

"Baking powder, tea, plum jam." Things she had been thinking about all summer filled her box.

"We have some nice English walnuts," suggested the clerk. "Can I sell you a sack?"

"Oh yes. And a length of that dotted cotton for curtains."

"And those kiddies would probably like some horehound candy."

"Okay. A nickels worth, please."

One purchase she saved for last. Embarrassed, she waited until the store owner's wife was on duty behind the counter.

"I need a pair of overalls, please."

"Size?"

"For me," stammered Sophie.

"Oh, of course," said the woman. "Several homesteading women have bought jeans for themselves lately. What's good for the gander is even better for the goose."

"Please," said Sophie. "I really need them."

"May I suggest a pair of bib overalls? They might be more comfortable for a woman in your condition."

Surprised that the clerk had noticed her swelling belly, Sophie bought an extra pair in a larger size for the months to come.

"A length of flannel to sew into baby things? I have some in yellow with little blue flowers."

Dragon Slaying and Angel Wings

~~~Klara~~~

Klara felt more at ease at the second meeting of the Canton Women's Sewing Club. She remembered several names and took her place at the long table with her project ready to proceed. Miss Birdie demonstrated several techniques for bringing the chalked outlines to life. She took a large eyed needle and threaded it with a heavy strand of metallic thread, then worked it back and forth to fill in the petals of a lily design. She edged the silver petals with gold thread and picked out the stems with a bright green.

"Oh. Long strokes. Much faster than embroidery."

"More like painting."

"See how the flowers are shaping up." She held the design for all to see. "Now for the stamens. They're formed with rows of tiny sequins. It's the details that will bring your picture to life."

While the other ladies worked their lily petals, Klara filled in the great silver horse on her picture. The work on the dragon and armor slowed her down a bit, but it gave her the chance to use a great variety of colors and textures.

"Miss Birdie, what will I do for the face and hands?"

"Good question. I've brought an example."

She unwrapped a large framed picture of a child with a lamb and held it for the class to see.

"Look. The face is cut from an old lithograph and stitched in place. The same for the bare arms of the child."

When Klara had finished the dragon's scarlet wings, Miss Birdie brought her a suitable bit of lithograph. She also brought an envelope which she emptied on the table.

"The sequins I promised. Angel faces with wings." She spread the metallic decorations on Klara's pattern. "They're large, so you can use them to fill up some of the empty places very quickly."

"Pink angels, silver and gold, too."

"They match the thread and they have little holes to stitch through."

"I'll put them in the corners. They can watch over Jorge."

By the time Klara finished her project she had ten angels flying watch. Other sequins, the little round ones, would decorate Jorge's cape and the horse's saddle pad.

"Good work class. Next week you can outline with gold thread," said Miss Birdie. "We'll make our pictures three dimensional. Mount and frame them, too."

~~~

"Looks like we have company," said Mrs. Lawrence. She pointed to the bike leaned against the fence.

"Torval, maybe," said Klara. "I wonder what he wants."

"Ah, the young men. They do want something, always."

Tillie met them at the front door. "I put him in the parlor. Hope that's okay?"

"Of course, Tillie," said Mrs. Lawrence. "Klara, see what he wants."

Klara found Torval pacing the small room, hat in hand. She asked him to sit down, then when he failed to explain himself, made all the inquiries she had learned from the language book. He answered distractedly that he was fine, his relatives were fine, the weather was lovely, his bike was operating perfectly.

When she got to his job, he burst out, "Klara, marry me. I'm going west."

"So soon? Why?" Now it was Klara's turn to pace around the parlor. She picked up small objects, examined them without seeing them, replaced them hap-hazardly.

"Come with me, Klara. It will be a fine adventure."

"We're too young. Babies still."

"I can take care of you. Work hard."

"Money. Do you have money?"

"Jack is coming. And Cousin Erik. He's been there before."

"And Tillie? Does she know?"

"We don't need Tillie. Please say yes, Klara."

"I send money home. They need me."

There was a polite knock on the door, then both Lawrences entered the room. "Let's all sit and discuss this rationally."

"Neither of you are old enough, legally or otherwise," said Mr. Lawrence. "I doubt if you have two dimes to rub together."

"My Uncle Jim will advance us the homestead filling fee," said Torval. "I have enough for the train fare."

"Food, nails, tar paper, tools, boots, work clothes. horse, harness, plow. Good grief! The list is a mile long."

"You marry and then come the babies. What do you know about babies, Torval?" said Mrs. Lawrence. "Even Klara knows nothing about babies."

"It would be cruel to drag our Klara along on your lark. Go by yourself. Get established, then come ask her if she wants to join you," Said Mr. Lawrence.

"My sister, Carrie, wants to join us," said Torval. "She'd be company."

"She wants to join you? Is she committed?" said Mrs. Lawrence.

"My mother is ill. She will stay with her until she's better."

Klara felt dazed as the arguments flew around her like a swarm of angry bees. The room was overflowing with pursing mouths, gesturing hands, and pacing feet. When Tillie appeared in the doorway with a sobbing child in her arms, she fled, relieved to have an escape. In the calm kitchen she soothed little Martin, kissed the bump on his forehead, and tried to explain the whole mess to Tillie.

"Nobody ask me," she said. "Help me, please."

"You don't have to do anything, Klara. Not a thing. Only what you choose."

Klara hugged Tillie until the child caught between them let out a yelp of protest. Klara released Tillie and danced the little Martin around the room. She stopped to hug Tillie again. Martin escaped and scooted for the parlor. Laughing with relief, Klara followed.

"Klara," said Mr. Lawrence. "How do you feel about going with Torval?"

"Not now. I stay. If it's all right with you."

"Of course, it's exactly right with us," said Mrs. Lawrence.

"I will make a deal with you, Torval," said Mr. Lawrence. "We stake you, give you a loan, help you finance this venture. You work hard, keep in touch with Klara, and return in a year. Ask her again if it still seems right."

Visibly deflated, Torval sat down. What could one eager boy do in the face of such determined opposition.

Mr. Lawrence sat down at the small desk in the corner and wrote several minutes. Two of the sheets he placed in envelopes and sealed them. The third he signed and handed to Torval.

"If you agree, add your signature to the bottom."

"It seems more than fair, sir."

"Give this one to the outfitter in Sioux Falls. It's a letter of credit. The owner is a friend of mine. This one is for the general store in Wall. You'll need it after you file your claim."

~~~

With all expectation of sweeping his girl off her feet with his grand plan dashed to bits Torval pedaled back to the station. Ambushed by a more sober plan, he vowed to work hard and show everyone he could succeed. By the time he lifted his bike down from the train in Sioux Falls doubts assailed him. What if Klara changed her mind. Or found another fellow while he was away. How could he possibly run off to the Rosebud without her. But, what would he do if he stayed without a job or a place to live. He was close to panic by the time he arrived at Jim and Ellen's place.

He parked his bike and let himself in the kitchen door.

Home on the Rage

~~~Sophia~~~

The days at the Lindblad homestead on the South Dakota prairie ground on. Hard work, tedium, plain food, isolation, small accomplishments, small tragedies. No one thing to give a body cause to snap, to rage against the universe, regret the day of their birth, not until the new baby came.

Full of pancakes and fried rabbit, the children played in the yard. Arvid sat on the bunk pulling on his boots. Sophie allowed herself a deep breath, poured a cup of coffee, then sat down at the kitchen table. Both table and benches were hewn from old logs and cast off lumber, the work of an itinerant carpenter in trade for a few nights lodging and half a bottle of whiskey.

"You should level these legs," said Sophie. "This table is unsteady."

"I need to go to Wall today," said Arvid.

"Not today. Please, Arvid."

"You can't tell me what to do."

"Arvid. The baby. It's time, I think."

"You said that last week." He grabbed his hat and stormed out. The sound of the horse's hooves drumming the hard pan soil proclaimed his departure.

For a few minutes anger drowned out Sophie's fear. She pounded her fists on the table and kicked the flimsy bench against the wall. When the tears came she collapsed on the bunk and cried her blanket wet. Exhausted, she dozed off until a cramping pain reminded her there was no escape. Relax, Sophie girl, she told herself. Maybe it's another false alarm. She dozed again and dreamed of a fierce bird determined to rip her to pieces. She woke with a start. A new pain gripped her as she struggled to the surface of consciousness.

Lily tugged on her sleeve.

"Sorry, Baby. Mama was having a bad dream."

"Mama, Mama. There's a lady."

Sophie struggled to prop herself up on the edge of the bunk.

"Tell her to come in, please, Lily."

Even while she grappled with the pain. Sophie took inventory of the dim room. The broken bench, dirty dishes, and grease encrusted pans stacked on the sheet metal stove made her forget everything for a minute. God, don't let it be that old biddie from the church society. The next second she would have welcomed the queen of England.

"Dearie me. You're a ripe one ain't you," said Mercy Lemmon. "Lily, take the child outside and get me some clean rags."

Sophie could hear muttering in the doorway. "You came back, Arvid."

"Not a chance. Your cowardly man was high-tailing it for Wall when he stopped to tell me you could use some help. That's my boy, Devon. A bit slow, but sweet as can be."

As the day wore into dusk, Mercy encouraged Sophia to scream and curse Arvid when the pains came sharp and close. Finally, the baby popped into the world, red and slippery, amidst Mercy Lemmon's nonstop talk, Devon's mutterings, and Sophie's cursing. A howling wind outside the poor soddy nearly drowned them all out.

"Is it a storm? I need to see to the children," said Sophie. She tried to push the new baby into Mercy's arms.

"Lie back," said Mercy. "Dev has them washed and fed. He's seeing to your livestock now."

"And Arvid?"

"Drink this, child. It's weak tea with honey."

"Where can he be?"

"His ears are burning, wherever he is."

Great Expeditions
When is a Lark not a Lark

~~~Torval~~~

Torval, Jack, and Cousin Erik spent most of the summer months preparing for their great homesteading adventure. A fly on the wall would have wondered if they really intended or wanted to go. They camped out in Jim's back yard with a canvas tent for shelter. Torval continued to make deliveries for his uncle in return. The three boys cooked their meals on an open camp fire though Aunt Ellen often took pity on them and provided instruction and whole meals. They repeatedly begged her to join them on their expedition.

"Think of all those ladies on the desolate prairie who crave a new hat," said Torval. "You could make loads of money."

"Silly boy." Ellen was patiently demonstrating the breaking of eggs into the cast iron skillet. "No shell in the pan. Prairie women have no money."

"They could trade you eggs. How is your mum, Torval?"

"I think we will have to leave without Carrie," said Torval.

"And soon, too," said Jack. "Winter will be here before we know it."

"I don't know about you fellers," said Erik, " but I'm catching the next emigrant train."

"Wish we could scrape up enough dough for a trip to the World's Fair," said Torval. "One last fling."

"He's nutso," said Erik. "Buffalo's the wrong direction."

"And we barely have two nickels to rub together."

"Definitely time to move west."

True to his word, Erik was packed and ready to move out the following Thursday. Jack and Torval gave Ellen and Jim a reluctant goodbye and followed suit. They joined a ragged group of would-be

124

landowners on the platform to board the train. They would leave the train at Murdo and hire a local to direct them to the remaining unclaimed land. The last thing Torval did was mail a postcard to Klara.

~~~

When Klara returned from sewing club where she had learned how to finish and frame her picture, she found a card and a letter waiting for her on the kitchen table. The card had a picture of the Canton railway station on one side and a brief note from Torval on the other side informing her that the homesteading party had left for Murdo. The letter bore a Swedish postmark.

C. M. & ST. P. DEPOT, CANTON, S. D.

"From your brother?"
"Ivar. He wants to come. Before winter if possible."
"He probably needs a letter of sponsorship. We'll wire it in the morning. Does he have enough money?"
"He says he save every penny we send. And he has a job that will take care of his ship passage."
"Job?"
"Like me. Nanny to old couple traveling to New York. Carry baggage. Buy tickets. Deliver them to waiting family."
"Resourceful fellow. Shouldn't be too hard to find him employment."

~~~

Though the boys had very little baggage, they elected to ride in the converted stock car stacked with household goods. Torval leaned back against his rucksack and watched the countryside slip by outside. His bike was wedged securely between an antique highboy and someone's recent purchase of window panes. All manner of things protruded from the wall of goods piled to the roof of the car. A stack of chicken crates was lashed to the wall by the door. The boys had been enlisted to keep an eye on the birds and cover them if the weather changed or they became too agitated.

"Gor, there's a lot of stuff here," said Jack. "Maybe we shoulda brought more."

Like Torval, he had settled on work clothes, tools, and a few cooking utensils. Erik had added a long rifle and two hand guns to his stash. On the advice of Uncle Jim Torval also had a bundle containing nails, candles, matches, a long knife, and whetstone. Ellen had added a sewing kit.

"Do you think we shoulda brought stamps and postcards?" said Jack. "I never even told Tillie I was leaving."

"There's a post office at Wall."

"Klara will tell her, but I thought you were done with Tillie?" said Torval.

"I thought so, but now I'm not so sure."

"If she thought you a sop before, she'll really think so now. Running off like this. Not a word of goodbye." said Erik.

"You should talk. Where's your girl?"

"Love em and leave em, I always say."

~~~

While the boys sat discussing their love life on the settler train rumbling across the prairie, the sponsorship letter wired by Mr. Lawrence arrived in Ludvika, Sweden. There the dispatcher woke up his son, gave him the printed message, and sent him on his way to Hagge. Ivar would have his sponsorship letter in time to meet the couple he was to accompany to New York.

~~~

Sophie paid Mercy Lemmon from her small stash and put the house in order. She refused to look at Arvid when he returned days later. With baby Will on her hip she slapped the noon meal on the table and motioned the children to bow their heads in a short table prayer. After a few hasty bites Arvid left the room. They could hear him busy at something in the yard, but paid him no mind.

Later in the day Arvid cut a place in the south facing wall and installed one of the precious windows hauled from Sioux Falls. A peace offering or penance for sin, who knew. The other window still leaned against the pig pen wall making a warm place for the yellow dog on sunny days.

~~~

As the train made its way across the prairie, it stopped at intervals to allow settlers to unload at places as close to their claims as possible. At each stop Erik, Torval, and Jack jumped out to help unload. By the time they reached Murdo the box car was nearly empty. The town was a sad jumble of shacks made from sod and scrap lumber. The two false front buildings proved to be the saloon and a railroad office which shared space with the only store in town.

"Gor. Maybe we shoulda stocked up before we left home," said Jack.

"We'll go to Wall after we find our land," said Erik. "Don't worry."

"Let's find our guide and get cracking," said Torval. "Not making any money standing here gawking."

The railroad man directed them to the saloon where they found a dusty looking man of about eighty. Old Pappy, as the locals called the guide, looked the boys over and spat into the dust of the dirt floor. He thumped his feet off the table and stood up.

"You got the money?"

"Yes sir." Jack counted out four quarters and a dozen dimes, then placed them on the table. "It's what you asked."

Old Pappy scooped up the coins and shambled out of the saloon.

"Horses," he said. "You got horses?"

"They said we could get them here," said Jack. "Buy or rent."

In a lean-to stable behind the saloon they found a motley collection of mounts. After much arguing they decided to rent a buckboard and a pair of sturdy bay geldings.

"That way we can take our time buying horses," said Jack.

"They'll be cheaper, too," said Erik. "These nags are way overpriced."

"And it'll give Torv a chance to see if his bike can tackle this rough country."

"No way," said Erik. "You gotta give in and get a horse, Torv."

They loaded the bike and their rucksacks, harnessed the horses, and went to pick up Old Pappy.

"You boys got food? Firewood? Water?"

"We need all that stuff?"

"Ain't nothin out on that prairie."

They stopped at the store and added a barrel of water, flour, bacon, coffee, and eggs to their stash. They topped off the load with bundles of firewood and tied Pappy's weathered horse to the tail gate. There was barely room for the old man in the loaded wagon.

"You, Torv, are elected to guard the eggs," said Erik. "I expect to have them safe and sound for breakfast."

That order proved to be a tall one as they bumped their way off the beaten path to the ford at Peach Creek. Torval finally decided to walk behind the slow moving group.

"Where's the creek?' said Erik.

"Dried to dust this time a year," said Pappy. "Banks are low here."

The boys sized up the rutted approach to the creek bed and voted to lead the team across. An hour later they passed a lop-sided soddy with a half finished out building in the distance. It looked deserted until a yellow dog raised its head from a pile of rubbish to bark at them.

"Someone actually lives here?" said Torval. "Looks like a dump."

"Whole family," said Pappy. "Keep to themselves mostly."

By dusk they had reached an area of low bluffs and strange wind carved formations. After winding their way down over the lip of a natural bowl formation Pappy announced their arrival. Their land began on the slopes of the bowl and fanned out onto the flat gravelly plain.

"Gor. Can you get any farther from civilization?"

"You wanted to get away from it all," said Pappy. "This here is the tail end of the section. No neighbors. Man would have to be crazy to want that land above you."

"Is any of it flat?"

"The hunting is good."

"We don't have a plow anyway."

"And winter is coming. Can't plant this time of year."

After they staked the near corners of the first claim Pappy advised them to make camp and finish the work in the morning. Then he wrapped himself in his slicker and went to sleep. The boys fashioned a tent from their canvas, made a small fire to brew coffee, and sat around chomping hard tack to the accompaniment of Pappy's snores until they could no longer stay awake.

Morning found them traipsing around the prairie piling rocks at the corners of each claim. Jack was aghast to discover how big 140 acres really was. Even Torval the farm boy had never considered what really comprised an acre.

"Do we have to plow all this, Pappy?" said Jack. "It's mostly shale."

"Ten acres, boy." said Pappy. "And you got a couple of years to do it."

"And build a house," said Erik.

"I'd advise you get some cattle come spring. Let 'em browse the spring grass and get them to market before summer. Quick turn over."

The badland homesteads seemed vast and empty when Pappy mounted his horse and rode off.

"Guess this is it, boys. Make or break time."

"Where do we start, Erik?"

"Shelter first. We'll bunk together for now."

"Can we cut a cave into the bluff?"

"Too many snakes. Let's lay out a rectangle and cut the sod, then we'll build up around the place we cut out. Understand?"

"How big?"

An afternoon of hard labor found the new soddy two layers high. They stretched the canvas over the top and slept in the dugout that night. Had they been less exhausted they might have worried about the night clamor of the prairie. Hoots, howls, wuffling, snorting, sharp cracks, the shuffling of distant wings, the padding of small footsteps, and the faint pulse that may have indicated human presence. The prairie was not a quiet place.

~~~

Sophie noted the passing of the Hanson party with little interest. It was all men with their boisterous talk and rented horses. By now she recognized the horses from the Murdo stable. Nags long past their prime. She dumped dry bread into the yellow dog's pan and added the whey from her morning's work of making cottage cheese. She noticed the yellow pup was no longer a pup. She knelt and prodded the dog's swollen belly and developing teats.

"What's wrong with Sadie?" said Lily. She had appeared at Sophie's side in silent curiosity.

"Nothing wrong, Lily," said Sophie. "She's going to have babies. We need to treat her nice. See that she gets plenty of food and water."

"She can have some of mine."

"No, sweet girl. You eat your whole share. Now let's make dinner."

When Arvid came in to eat, he joked with the children and tried to engage Sophie in conversation. She ignored him and dished up the rabbit stew and biscuits.

"I found a neighbor willing to loan me his breaking plow."

"Why. Papa?"

"So we can plant crops. Maybe try winter wheat."

Sophie broke her silence. "Who's going to pull it? Not our poor horse."

"I'm working on it. He has a team to rent. Some sort of trade."

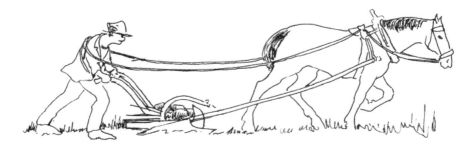

A few days later there was a great clamor from the yard.

"Mommy, Mommy come see," said Lily. "Papa has a horse, two horses."

"Lordy, lordy," said Sophie. She ran out to see what was happening.

Grinning like a circus clown Arvid sat astride a sturdy horse complete with collar and harness. He had its mate on a lead line with the breaking plow in tow. What he had offered the distant neighbor wasn't mentioned. Sophie returned to her task of churning butter and Arvid set to turning the reluctant earth.

The parcel of land broken by the previous homesteader had grown up in rank wheat grass. He began there. The ground was dry, but yielded to the plow eventually. By sundown he had a noticeable portion plowed dark against the pale prairie grass. The unbroken land was a different matter. After two or three trips up and down the uneven field both Arvid and the horses were shaking with exhaustion.

Sophie met them at the end of the row with a jug of water. Arvid took a long drink, then poured the rest over his head.

"It can't be done, Sophie. At this rate it'll take years."

"We'll do with what we have."

"No choice. Lily, unhook the traces."

Free of the plow the horses wandered to the scant shade cast by the soddy. Sophie found a bucket and gave them a drink. After the sun went down Arvid led them home. The clank and scrape of the plow could be heard long after they disappeared from sight.

Inside, Lily hurried to start the cooking fire, while Sophie sat in the much abused rocker. She nursed baby Will and held little Mattie tight beside her. What's to become of us, she wondered.

~~~

Klara, too, was wondering about her future. Ivar had arrived on the morning train from Chicago. Their embrace on the platform had been awkward. Klara couldn't remember ever hugging her brother and would have settled for a brief handshake. Tillie, who had tagged along in case there was baggage to tote, pushed Klara forward and demanded they greet each other more effusively.

"He won't bite you, girl," she said. "Like this." She hugged the young man and kissed him on both cheeks. "There. Welcome to America, Ivar."

He stammered his thanks. The girls grabbed his trunk, one on each handle, and escorted him from the station. Tillie pointed out various things along the way, while Klara interjected a bit of translation now and then. In a few minutes they were home.

The Lawrences met them at the door and spoke to Ivar in Norwegian. They explained about the job with a nearby farmer. After dinner they would harness the horse and deliver him to his new home. Much to Tillie's distress the conversation was mostly in Norwegian which both Klara and Ivar understood though imperfectly. Mr. Lawrence explained that both he and his wife had immigrated years before.

"This farmer. He is a hard man?" said Ivar. "Demanding?"

"Old Rolf? No, he's pretty easy going. Likes his whiskey, plays cards."

"He has much land?"

"Enough. He raises grain. Wheat mostly. Fattens a few head of cattle."

"I don't know about those things," said Ivar. "Picking rocks I know."

"Not to worry. Mostly he needs a strong back and willing hands."

"He has no sons to work his land?"

"He's a bachelor. Won't have a woman on his place. You may have to do the cooking too."

"Ah. That I know. I cook for the school this last year. In trade for tuition."

"You're interested in education?" said Mrs. Lawrence. "You should get your certificate and teach. The township schools are in dire need of teachers."

"She's a school teacher," said Klara. "Very smart."

"Get settled at Rolf's and learn English. We'll talk more later."

~~~

By the time the first snow covered the dry prairie Erik, Torval, and Jack had a sturdy house two blocks thick and high enough to stand up in. They had found their way to the bustling town of Wall where they discovered a bargain in used lumber. They spent some of

Torval's credit for tar paper and nails. The house would have a pitched roof made water tight with tar paper and a layer of sod.

"How about windows," said Jack. "Let in light."

"Let in cold too," said Erik. "Maybe we should save windows for spring."

"Here's a real door. It should keep the cold out."

"The bone yard of hope," said Torval. "All this salvage. Every piece represents someone's failure."

"Ah, the boy is a philosopher," said Erik. "Does your door have a knob?"

"Yes. No hinges though."

"We'll cut some, out of leather," said Torval. "Yes, Jack. Make your own. You shoulda stayed on the farm a bit longer. Learn all the tricks."

"That's about all that will fit on the wagon. Let's get cracking."

Wake in Bitter Darkness

Winter gave little warning that year. It hit the badland plains with full fury. Cattle out of sight of their shelter simply drifted before the wind heads down, tails tucked. Many fell to their death over the gullies and cliffs that streak this land. Others met barriers of fence or rock face and were smothered by those that followed. For three days the wind howled and snow piled deep. The Lindblad soddy, built on the open plain, caught the brunt of the storm and was soon covered to its eaves. Sophie could only hope that the cow and chickens were safe in their shed. It was impossible to cross the yard to care for them. The children and the yellow dog had come running to the house at the first blast of snow. Arvid was away on one of his business trips.

Sophie fed the children left over stew and gave the scraps to the dog. Then she bundled them into bed with her and told them it would be all better tomorrow. When they awoke a fine sift of snow covered the bed quilts.

"Stay put. I'll get the fire going."

The yellow dog wiggled free and barked her need. When Sophie tried to let her out, the drift of snow made it impossible to open the door. The dog shivered and cowered awhile before she relieved herself in the far corner of the soddy. Sophie covered the mess, then dug a shallow trench along the wall. The children would need it next.

The breakfast fire warmed the house. Sophie made pancakes and set a pot of corn meal to cooking. Flavored with bacon grease it would keep hunger from the door for several days. Yesterday's milk sat on the table. A thick layer of cream had risen to the top. She had baked bread the day before and they had jam and butter. At least they wouldn't go hungry.

By the second morning the stench from the makeshift privy

they had dug in the far corner pervaded every inch of the house. The stack of firewood had dwindled to a few poor sticks. They ate a cold breakfast, then huddled together under the pile of down quilts. By noon Sophie thought the wind had let up some. She crawled out of the nest of blankets, pulled on her work boots, and warned Lily to keep care of the babies.

Sophie put her shoulder to the door and managed to wedge it open a few inches. Snow cascaded around her, but she pushed the shovel into the crack and worked it up through the drift. When it broke through the frozen crust, a new stream of snow assaulted her. It was still snowing and howling outside. The drifts had simply insulated them from the noise and belching of the prairie storm.

Lily poked her head out of the quilts. "Is it better, Mama?"

"No," said Sophie. "I need to pull this door to. Come help."

In a shower of snow they managed to close the door. Sophie collected the snow in the dish pan and bucket. "We might need it later, Lily."

The day drew to a close in an agony of boredom broken only by fits of crying from the children and makeshift meals. Sophie had broken up the bench and used it for firewood. She was trying to figure out how to dissemble the table when the yellow dog began pacing and whimpering, circling, flopping down on the floor, biting her flanks, leaping up to pace some more.

"What's wrong with her, Mama?"

"I don't know." said Sophie. When she tried to touch the dog, it snapped at her. "Let her be."

They watched the addled creature from their nest of quilts until Lily fell asleep. Sophie extracted herself from the heap of children and bedding, tucked baby Will in beside Lily, and went to the hooks on the wall that served as her closet. She found the old dress ruined that first day on the prairie and folded it into a bed for the dog. She placed it in the corner near the stove. The yellow dog, quiet now, circled a few times and plopped down. The first tiny pup arrived a few minutes later. By the time the children awoke six more pups had joined their sibling and were pushing and squirming to find the best position at the new mama's teats.

Around noon they heard a great racket outside. Sophie and

Lily tried the door again and were relieved to hear an answer to their shouts. The Hanson boys were in the yard shoveling a passage way through the drifts. By evening the Lindblad home had been set to rights. The cow, though miserable, had been fed and milked. The frantic chickens had survived and were cackling and scratching away at the dry bread Lily and Matty spread out on the tamped snow around the shed. The job of mucking out the soddy fell to Sophie while Erik played with baby Will. Torval and Jack made the yellow dog and her pups comfortable in the empty pig pen.

"We could have one of these fellers when he gets old enough," said Torval.

"Wonder if he'd hunt," said Jack. "Sniff out game."

"We could teach him."

"Miz Lindblad," said Torval. "Any chance we could have a pup?"

"Come back in a few months and pick one out."

The Last Best West

Shake Up, Make Up, Move On

~~~*Klara*~~~

Klara received several postcards and one long rambling letter from Torval over the winter. Her replies were short and mainly news of the children in her charge. The boys were thriving and into everything. The oldest would soon be off to school and Klara wondered if her job would end then. When she mentioned her uncertainty to Torval, he fired off a plea for her to join him.

For a short while she envisioned herself in her own little bungalow in a woodland setting. Tall pines and wildflowers, a clear stream, deer that crept up to the door stoop to graze, and birds trilling in the bushes sent a wave of homesickness washing over her. Tillie quickly pulled the curtain over Klara's fantasy home with a photo card she had received from Jack.

"This, this is where the boys are living." She pushed the card into Klara's hands. "Do you see any trees? Even one?"

"No, no trees."

"Birds? Grass even? Nothing but shale and dirt. And look at that house. One room with three men living in it. You'd be their own personal slave. Cooking and mucking up dirt day after day."

Klara put Torval's card away unanswered.

~~~

Spring brought a blush of green to the prairie. Grass grew knee high. Every knoll and hollow had a carpet of wild flowers. Goldenpea and starlily brightened the open banks and eroded slopes, while drifts of gumbo lily turned the hillsides a soft white. Hoards of newly hatched prairie chicks scuttled about scratching for insects.

The women hauled beds, tables, benches, trunks into the yard and proceeded to clean the grime of winter from their homes. Walls were given a new coat of clay mud from the creek beds. Some whitewashed those walls when the clay dried, others hung new material to cover the dirt walls. Dirt floors were swept and pounded smooth. Everything that could be washed went into the boiling wash pots in the yard. Work pants, socks, shirts, gloves, linen towels, and curtains were stirred clean and hung to dry on clothes lines across the prairie.

The men hardly noticed except when they were given a cold meal and ordered to eat in the yard. Every muscle and sinew of man and beast was engaged in breaking the soil and getting seed into the ground. Arvid managed to plow a few more acres before he gave up again. He seeded the plowed land to oats, brought home a pair of piglets, and settled in to work for a neighbor.

Sophie sold the remaining puppies and rejoiced that the yellow dog was pregnant again. She had kept her hidden stash of money from running out by selling eggs from her growing flock of chickens, but the yellow pups proved to be an even better money source. Dogs were scarce on the prairie in those early days.

A few miles past the Lindblad soddy Jack and Erik spent much of their spare time training their new dog. Torval had opted out of dog ownership and worked on his bike instead. He had found that under inflating his tires made it possible to tackle the smoother sections of the prairie. They had sent their small herd of cattle to market in the nick of time. The beasts were still plump and slick coated though the grass had dried to dust. Plowing seemed impossible and another winter highly undesirable.

"What say we blow this place," said Erik. "We're money ahead."

"Can we sell?" said Jack. "We've paid the filing, built a fair house."

"Where would we go?" said Torval. "Can't see us going back east."

"I hear they're opening new land up north. Near the Montana line."

"We could get in on the better land."

"Be first, instead of the tail end," said Torval. "Maybe Klara will join me."

"And Tillie and Carrie. Some women would ease the pain of our cooking."

"And the stink of your socks."

"What socks? I burned them."

"Seriously, boys, let's pack up and see if we can find a sucker in Wall to take this place off our hands."

~~~

On the Lindblad homestead the land sowed to oats had received the spring rains gladly. The green blades flourished under the summer sun and all seemed well, until it was time for the grain to head out.

"This wind will never stop," grumbled Arvid. "And this damned swill. Can't you cook something beside fry bread and eggs?"

"The yeast starter went bad. It's the heat," said Sophie. "No bacon either."

"I suppose you want me to haul water again, too."

"You promised to get the well digger out from town."

Arvid dumped his plate on the floor and stomped out. A few minutes later they heard the drum of hooves as he left the yard.

"Where's Papa going," said Lily.

"Town probably. Let's clean up this mess. Take the scraps to the chickens."

~~~

The moisture in the soil was soon gone. The oats, buffeted by hot winds, were on the verge of drying up. Desperate to save something, they cut the ten acres by hand and stacked it as hay. A neighbor offered six dollars for the entire crop if they would haul it to his barn and fork it into the loft. That figured out to sixty cents an acre. They decided keep their hay to feed the milk cow and her calf through the next winter.

"Maybe we should move on," said Sophie one morning at breakfast.

"Now look who wants to move," said Arvid. "Old homebody, herself."

"Sell this place to a big family. Workers. We can't do it, Arvid."

"We could run cattle here. Or sheep even."

"Takes money, lots of money, to get started."

"It's always money, isn't it? You should have married a rich man."

"Lily needs to start school."

"I'll think about it."

Arvid was working for a neighbor that week picking corn for a penny a bushel. The week before he helped another neighbor put up an earthen dam. Before that he joined a work crew to dig wells near the county line. For each job he was gone from home for a week or more, eating with the family who hired him, sleeping in their barns or sheep wagons. He admitted himself that he enjoyed the visiting, the eating, and the whisky immensely.

~~~

Back in Canton Klara and Tillie washed and pressed small shirts and shorts, matched up socks, and arranged a week's wardrobe for the oldest Lawrence boy. The first day of school was at hand.

"You're nervous as an old hen, Klara."

"He doesn't need me anymore."

"There's still the baby."

"The 'baby' is practically running the household." As if to demonstrate, the youngest Lawrence appeared at Klara's elbow with a wrinkled shirt and a demand for instant pressing. "See. He wants his shirts done up too."

"Maybe you still want to join Torval?"

"Have you heard from Jack?"

"They're moving to a better place. Away from the badlands. Does Ivar talk about moving west?"

"Always. Always the dream."

"Plan now and make the move in the spring. The two of you."

"You could come with us, Tillie. You don't need Jack."

"It would be a great adventure."

~~~

The spring sun blared full on through the nursery windows. Every speck of dust, every scuff mark and dirt blotch screamed clean me, scrub me, wipe and polish. Klara wielded the damp mop and duster with fury. Torn with indecision, she tried to blot out her thoughts with work. Torval's letter lay open on the nursery table, a giant, glowing missive that demanded her attention, her yea or nay, her very future.

Dear Klara, she had read. *We have found a buyer for our badland place. I will be in Canton to see my father on the 28th. If you have any feelings for me, now is the time. We can be married before we head to Sioux territory to make a home of our own. I hope to persuade Carrie to join us. Yours Truly, Torval*

"How can he ask like that," muttered Klara. She rubbed the glass of the break-front until the China cups inside rattled their protest.

~~~

The young people congregated in the front room of Mr. Hanson's small Canton house. When the talk and laughter rose above normal chatter, they spilled out into the yard. Jack, doing his best to charm Tillie, expounded on the prairie's charm, the distant mountains, the carpets of wild flowers, all manner of little creatures to amuse and entertain. Tillie countered with questions about running water and electricity. Klara said little, but listened intently when her brother, Ivar, questioned Erik and Torval about the homestead process. Torval had not mentioned marriage and seemed oblivious to her presence. It wasn't until the group broke up to go their separate ways that he addressed her.

"How about it, Klara?" he said. "Are you in?"

"In? What does it mean?" Klara pulled away and walked off towards the Lawrence house.

"You better follow her if you're talking about what I think you are," said Jack.

"That's no way to propose to a lady, Torv." said Erik.

"Damn," said Torval. He rushed off into the darkness. "Klara, stop. Listen to me. Please."

"Big idiot," said Erik. "You think he'll ever grow up."

~~~

The marriage ceremony took place in the clerk's office in Sioux Falls. Jack and Torval's sister, Carrie, stood up with the couple. Klara had wanted Tillie to be there for her, but Mrs. Lawrence had a meeting at the college and needed her to stay with the children.

Only the girl at the front desk noticed Klara's agitation. Before the two couples entered chambers, she put her hand on Klara's sleeve. "Are you sure about this, Honey?"

Klara nodded dumbly and followed Torval. The ceremony was a blur of mumbled words and signed documents, but still felt like it went on for hours. Klara was surprised to discover the sun still hovered overhead when they emerged from the court house. Torval clutched her elbow and guided her to the buggy with an unfamiliar proprietary air.

Torval dropped Klara at the Lawrence house with a quick kiss. "Next Tuesday. Be packed and ready."

Before Klara could answer Mrs. Lawrence drove up. "Did you do it, Klara? Did you tie the knot?"

"Knot? What knot?"

"Marriage, did you really marry this young fellow?"

"That she did," said Torval with a tinge of pride in his voice. "Signed, sealed, and delivered. We leave for the last great west next Tuesday."

"I had hoped we could give you a proper wedding reception."

"That's very nice of you, but we need to move along."

"Photos. You must have a proper wedding photo."

"Oh yes," said Klara. "A picture to send home. For my family."

Torval looked at Klara, really looked at her for the first time that day. She had been so quiet, she had barely intruded on the whirl of plans in his head.

"Of course you should have photographs. I'm so sorry. I didn't think."

"Come by Saturday, Torval. Wear your tux. Rent or borrow one. I'll have Klara ready and we'll take care of that detail. It will be our wedding present to you."

"Thank you. That's very kind," said Torval. "See you then, Klara."

"Come, Klara," said Mrs. Lawrence. "Let's get you a dress."

"Shopping? We go shopping?"

The thought brought up terrifying images of shopping with Tillie. With Tillie it had been a marathon. They had traipsed to numerous shops, argued with reluctant sales clerks, hemmed and hawed over fit and color and price in endless debate.

"What about the children?"

"Tillie can handle things a bit longer."

Acquiring a suitable dress with Mrs. Lawrence proved easier than Klara believed possible. She guided Klara to the open buggy and urged the horse towards downtown.

At the small shop they were greeted like royalty and escorted to a back room and seated on a gilt settee. Tea and small cakes were produced while Mrs. Lawrence explained their mission. Klara was measured and patted and viewed from every angle to determine how best to transform her into a glowing bride.

"Not white though," said Mrs. Lawrence. "She may wish to wear this gown for other occasions."

Swatches of color appeared for Klara's examination. With the help of her entourage she narrowed her choices to three. Lilac, forest green, and Bordeaux red were produced in the form of rolls of material.

"Stand here," said the sales woman. "Yes. Face me now."

She artfully draped the lilac material over Klara's shoulders and up against her throat. "Now, then, turn around."

She was examined under the shop lights, by the sunlight streaming in a window, and in a dim light approximating the subdued lighting of an intimate meeting place.

"No," said Mrs. Lawrence. "It makes you look liverish."

"I agree," said the shop lady. "Makes you look yellow. Forget Lilac."

The forest green was better, but seemed harsh in daylight.

"Too dark. Makes you look pale."

To Klara's relief the red proved nearly perfect, but if she thought that was the last of the choices, she was sadly mistaken.

"Now for the style. Bring the book Lizebeth."

Klara was soon inundated with bishop sleeves and high standing collars, yokes and tucks, plaits and cuffs and hems. Ruffles and ruching, flounces, binding, and piping. Mrs. Lawrence made short work of these choices by authorizing a high collar with rows and rows of tiny pleats, puffy sleeves, and open work embroidery down the front.

"Make the waist separate from the skirt. Give us one of those white lawn ones, too. She can change the look of the outfit by changing tops."

"Perhaps one of the plainer ones," said the shop owner. "She can dress it up with ribbons or jewelry as she pleases."

"And a plain skirt, too. One of the gray melton cloth ones."

"With a hem flounce? Or walking length?"

"The shorter one, please."

"Very good. It will give good wear."

"You can have everything ready on Friday?"

"For you, yes."

After they bought shoes and hose Mrs. Lawrence suggested they stop at the milliner's, but Klara refused the idea of a fancy hat.

"Flowers, then. We'll order a corsage and a hair ornament. You'll be quite splendid."

And splendid she was standing with Torval in front of the painted photographer's back drop. Torval, himself, was dashing with his light hair parted in the middle and combed back.

"Ah, nice," said the photographer. "Now stand a bit closer together. Closer. The ladies don't bite, sir. At least not at first."

Even with the efforts of the wise cracking photographer, the couple managed to look sober and old for their tender years. He settled for dignified with a hint of the regal and called the session successful.

"When will the proofs be ready?"

"Next week sometime."

"Maybe before Tuesday?"

"Perhaps, yes, but maybe not."

"Mrs. Lawrence will come to choose," said Klara. "She knows good picture."

~~~

In the chill hour before dawn Ivar carried Klara's trunk to the buckboard. "This is the trunk James painted before you left home," said Ivar. "He did a good job."

"And Grandfather before him. See the flower designs." She traced the complex whorls and petals on the lid with her finger.

Goodbyes had been said the night before. A copy of the precious wedding photo awaited mailing on the Lawrence's sideboard. Neither Klara, nor Ivar had heard from home for many months and an aura of uncertainty invaded their excitement over this new great adventure.

"Do you think anyone will know where we are, Klara?"

"They say the post is quite good here."

"We don't even know where we will be."

"I see you brought paints and brushes. I thought only James was an artist."

"I found I'm fairly good at it. Painting, that is. Little scenes and such."

"You can paint our new home."

Home on the Plains

The Hanson party rode the train as far as Evarts where the train crew helped them unload wagons, goods, and livestock. For a group of homesteaders expecting to set up housekeeping they were lightly equipped. Klara and her brother, Ivar, had trunks and a bag apiece. Torval brought his bike, a few tools, his diaries, and clothing. Erik had an arsenal of rifles, pistols, and knives. Jack had a trunk, tools, and the yellow pup on a rope. Except for a few tin plates and a cast iron Dutch oven, no one had thought to bring household items. They had two spoons and three forks between them.

"Is there a general store?"

"Yes, sir. Evarts has about anything you need and even a few of the things you want."

"I'll work some of the kinks out of these horses," said Erik. "You all get the supplies."

Klara found the store with its creaking wooden floor unbelievably small. Shelves crammed with an assortment of goods ran floor to ceiling. Barrels of flour, sugar, and something pickled crowded around the counter. A small selection of hard goods was jammed between boxes of baking soda and washing powder. The prices chalked on the items made her gasp.

"Torval, can we afford any of this?"

"Pick out what you need most and we'll see."

"Flour, salt, sugar, and baking powder for sure. Spoons, mugs, a mixing bowl, sugar."

"Bacon and dry beans," said Torval. "And seed."

While Torval added seed grain to their pile, Klara picked out small packets of cucumber, squash, and pumpkin with a tiny envelope of hollyhock seed.

"Cheese. Can we afford a wedge of cheese? It should keep in

this dry country."

"Whatever you think we can use. I hope we can get chickens when we get settled."

Jack squeezed into the tiny store and reminded Torval to buy nails. They discussed the sort of nail that would best serve until the shop keeper informed them he had only one choice. He recommended they all buy leather work gloves and brought out a large selection from the back. "These should fit the lady. And you might consider getting her some britches, too."

Torval was horrified at the idea, but Klara accepted the offer to step to the shop keepers home next door to try on an assortment of overalls. She seemed quite happy with her selection and carried her purchase to the wagon. There was enough room in her trunk to pack her new britches next to her tissue-wrapped wedding gown. She tucked the flower seeds alongside.

Heading West

Joined by several other families they camped a scant few miles from Evarts the first night. Though the weather was perfect, they lashed a canvas tarp on either side of the wagon and constructed two shelters, one for Torval and Klara, the other for Erik, Jack, and Ivar. They cooked over an open fire and entertained themselves with songs and stories spiced by the addition of their traveling companions.

Such diversions, along with the excitement of a new adventure, made the journey flow quickly. The evening of the third day they recognized the quirky rock formations that marked the boundary of Butte County, the location of their new home.

"What are these weird rocks?" said Jack. "They look like trees."

"They are trees," said Erik. "Petrified trees."

"I'd rather have some real live ones," said Klara. "Does anything grow here?"

"Grass," said Erik. "Good for cattle and buffalo."

Klara thought of her packet of hollyhock seed and wondered if she should have brought more. Maybe Mrs. Lawrence or Tillie would send her some. Aloud she asked about the post office.

"There's one at Date. We should be in that area tomorrow or the next day."

The next day the party met up with one of the cattle ranchers in the area and received directions to Owl Creek, the first of the local landmarks. Streams were running high with spring rain and the area seemed lush with grass and wild flowers.

"Looks promising," said Erik. "Grass and water."

"The cows will like it anyway," said Torval. "If we had any cows."

"Are we getting cows?" said Klara. "A milk cow would be nice."

"Not me," said Torval. "I hate the beasts."

"Should be good hunting," said Erik. "I hear there's a coal seam down past Rabbit Creek, too."

"Coal?" said Ivar.

"Yeah. That black stuff you dig out of the ground. Keeps your house warm."

"Maybe we'll all become miners."

"Digging?" said Torval. "Definitely not the life for me"

"Digging and cutting sod. You, boy, are in for some real work."

After the group staked out their new home sites Torval found that he did have digging in his future. At Klara's suggestion the couple laid the outline of their house on an up sweeping portion of land that would save considerable labor.

"Dig out the sod blocks here and the back of the house will be underground."

"Twice the wall for half the labor."

"Warmer too."

"Let's hope there's no rock under here." Torval plunged the long sod cutting knife into the virgin soil. With a sawing motion he cut a grid of potential blocks along a twelve foot section of prairie. Freeing the first blocks proved to be tedious and frustrating. Torval's careful plan dissolved in a frenzy of hacking and shoveling. The first blocks finally emerged much disheveled and barely discernable from random lumps of dirt. With Klara's help he rolled the three foot blocks into place and sat down to rest.

"The next row should be easier."

"Is that Jack?" said Klara. "There, to the north."

"Looks like he has a team and plow."

Jack had borrowed a breaking plow from a neighbor and made short work of cutting the long sides of Torval's blocks.

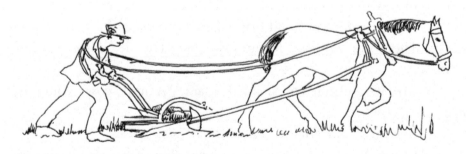

"That should save some time," said Jack. "I'll go cut Erik and Ivar's now."

"Thanks," said Torval. "Come back for supper. Klara should have something ready about sundown."

By supper time they had laid two courses of blocks brick style and a third row cross-wise for strength. The sod house was beginning to take shape. They could just see Ivar's soddy off in the distance. Erik and Jack's homestead lay on the other side of a long prairie swale to the west. Though it would have made sense to combine their efforts, the homestead laws mandated individual homes on each claim. Erik was not interested in acquiring land so he threw in his lot with Jack. Guns and iron work were more his style. He would soon find ample work shoeing horses and repairing all manner of equipment.

By week's end the three sod houses were ready to be roofed. After some spirited discussion about a flat roof versus a pitched roof they agreed to work together to raise this final defense against the elements. It quickly became apparent that the roof supports would have to run the short dimension of the building. No tree or piece of lumber could be found long enough for a ridge pole.

"By gor. What this country needs is a lumber mill," said Jack.

"Trees would help. I think they've all been used up."

"Or petrified. No forest has grown here in a million years."

"You exaggerate. Nothing is a million years old," said Torval.

"A lot you know. Didn't they teach you anything in school?"

~~~

Their Habitation Became Desolate

~~~Sophia~~~

Had Arvid listened to his wife's plea, they might have avoided the failures of several crop seasons. They planted corn, a new variety said to be impervious to heat and drought. Unfortunately they had to cut it when the ears were short and milky. It was the only way to avoid a total loss from an onslaught of powder black fungus. Though warned not to, they fed it to the cow through the winter and in the spring she dropped a dead calf.

Milo fared no better than oats. It flourished full and green, until the hot winds began to blow out of the badlands. What remained wasn't even salvageable for fodder. As a last resort, they sowed the ground to flax, a crop familiar to them from their homeland. For a few months the sturdy stalks withstood heat and draught. The Lindblads, along with neighbors who had joined them in the experiment, rejoiced.

Sophie stood on the small knoll examining the progress of the crop. Baby Will played at her feet. Lily and Matty held her hands.

"Can we eat now?" said Matty. "I want cake."

"Silly. You can't have cake until we go to town," said Lily.

"That treat was a mistake," said Sophie. "Poor baby. Gave you a taste for pleasures out of reach."

On their last trip to Wall Sophie had taken the children to the hotel dining room for tea and cake. A rare event and a first for little Matty. He had declined the fizzy root beer after one sip, but the tiny frosted cakes had left him begging for more.

"When's Papa coming home?' said Lily.

"I don't know," said Sophie. "He's working over towards the Black Hills."

Arvid had developed a bit of a reputation as a guide for the various people who showed up to see how folks lived on the prairie.

A busy rancher or a hard working homesteader would send a buckboard or a spring wagon to fetch him and Arvid would be off to show well-dressed easterners the strange formations of the badlands, the herds of antelope grazing the high plateau, the rustic towns of Wall and Wasta. Sometimes he was commissioned to take visitors as far as the Black Hills, a three or four day journey where the party would sleep in tents and eat around a cheery campfire. All provided by the rancher, of course. Arvid was well fed, but paid little for his services.

"Well, he needs to come home," said Lily. "He promised to build a play house."

"And a swing," said Matty.

"Your papa makes a lot of promises,"

Sophie had argued and raged at him for leaving them alone, but he ignored her. It was all a great lark for him.

"What's that, Mama?" said Lily. "That cloud way over there."

"I don't know. It seems to be moving."

"Is it a fire?"

"I don't think so. The color is off."

As they stood watching, the cloud moved closer. It swayed and dipped, then spread across the horizon. Low to the ground it seemed to be a living thing.

"Hoppers, Mama." said Lily. She shook a few from her clothes and ran for the house. Matty followed.

"It can't be," screamed Sophie. "We can't stand anymore." She shook her fists at the sky and cursed God and Arvid and the grasshoppers. When the cloud of insects filled the air and blackened the sky, she grabbed the baby and ran.

In the house she plucked the sharp winged creatures from their clothing and hair. Matty stomped them and scooped them into the slop bucket. Lily refused to help and hid herself under the bed quilts. When the chaos inside the house subsided, they could hear the creatures outside bashing themselves against the walls. They ate a cold supper and crawled into bed. Even the walls of the soddy and the thick quilts could not shut out the noise, the sound made by the rape of the prairie.

~~~

When Arvid returned to his family and the desolate fields, he finally realized there was no future on the Lower Brule. They had to move on. When he told Sophie about the grasslands north of the Black Hills, it sparked a bit of hope that grew as they packed up their battered possessions. Arvid managed to find a buyer interested in the soddy for a hunting shack. In a fit of contrition he gave the money to Sophie to hold. By week's end they were on their way.

Bittersweet Reunion

~~~Klara and Sophia~~~

Klara was busy mixing clay mud to chink the spaces between the sod blocks when she heard a horse in the yard. Wiping the clay from her hands, she stepped outside. Aware that she was alone, she approached the disheveled horseman slowly. The horse was a rib-thin mustang and the rider looked like a rag bag. She gasped when the rider dismounted. It was a woman with a child bundled in her arms.

"Please help me," said the woman.

"Sophie," said Klara. "Are you Sophie Lindblad?"

For an instant Sophie forgot her desperate situation. "Klara! Is it really you?"

Klara grabbed the horse's bridle before it could wander off. "What's wrong?"

"Snake bite. My son." Sophie thrust the child towards Klara.

"Bring him over here. In the wagon bed. There's some shade."

"Arvid is away. Working on the railroad the other side of Hettinger."

"He leave you alone? You look like baby is ready to come."

"Is there a doctor anywhere?"

Klara shrugged and examined the moaning child.

"Talusa told me stories about snake bite," babbled Sophie.

"Stories don't help. Who is this Talusa?"

"Talusa lived in bayous. In the south. Snake root and kerosene. We need snake root and kerosene."

"Torval will be here soon. Maybe he knows."

"Do something, anything."

Desperate, Klara made a poultice of dried sorrel leaves and vinegar.

"What is this sorrel?" said Sophie.

"For the stomach ache," said Klara. "And worms, I think. It's all we have."

"Poor baby. God help us."

"How many children do you have, Sophie?"

"You know Lily and Matty. Then there's Will here. And the new one." She patted her belly.

Poor Will. His little foot and leg swelled up huge before the fellows returned. He had screamed all afternoon. Nothing could quiet him. Exhausted, he finally fell into a stupor near sundown. Erik cut slits in the boy's skin to let the poison out and applied more sorrel. When all else seemed to have no effect, they carried the boy to the creek and laid him in the icy cold water.

By God's grace and in spite of human intervention Will survived the night. In the morning Erik harnessed the team, tied the skinny mustang to the tail gate and drove Sophie and Will home. There was nothing more they could do.

Arvid met them in the yard. "Where you been, woman?" When he learned that Will had been snake bit and that Sophie had killed the snake, he ranted at her for not salvaging the snake skin. Worth a dollar stretched and dried, he said.

Erik untied the mustang, looped the lead rope over a nearby post and wished Sophie good luck before he drove off.

Back home he gave a brief accounting to his friends. "That Arvid is a piece of work."

"What about Will?" said Klara.

"He seemed better. Kids are tough."

"This country needs a doctor."

~~~

Within the month dozens of sod buildings, houses and livestock shelters rose out of the prairie like odd little mushrooms. Erik joined a group of cattlemen to persuade a well digger to begin work on a common water source. While the well digger concentrated on finding water, Erik and a crew of homesteaders dug a holding pond and built a low dam. Both Rabbit Creek and Owl Creek would soon be dry for the season, but the area named Coal Springs held promise.

Torval and Jack studied the Sears and Roebuck catalogue for several days before they sent off an order for two galvanized water tanks. Even before the well came in they received notice to pick up their merchandise at the Hettinger rail head. Jack, Ivar, and Erik hitched up the team and set off on the three day trip. They promised Klara that the next purchase would be a *'princess reservoir cook stove'* guaranteed to burn wood or coal and complete with a porcelain lined reservoir.

With her cooking duties much reduced Klara plastered the interior of the dirt walls with the same clay mixed with ashes used to chink the blocks. Once she had the walls smooth and dry she hung the extra bed quilts in the corner where they had built a bed with a rope mattress. From her trunk she unwrapped the picture made at the sewing circle in Canton. She hung the dragon slayer by the door and seemed pleased with the spot of bright color in the drab room. Maybe the young knight on the pudgy horse could keep pestilence from the home.

As long as the weather held, they cooked and ate outside. The insects, especially flies, plagued them equally, inside or out. They had cut openings for windows in the front and side walls, but had not yet filled or covered them.

"Do you think they'll get back today?' said Klara. "It's been a week now."

"Expect the trip home will be slower," said Torval. "Or maybe they tied one on in Hettinger."

"Ivar doesn't drink."

"Neither does Erik, but this prairie life changes people."

Around noon they spotted a bit of dust on the northern horizon. It moved steadily closer until they were sure it was the returning travelers. Torval uncovered his bike and took off to greet them. Klara built up the fire and put the coffee pot on to boil.

Covered with dust, but jubilant, the four young men entered the yard with the loaded wagon. The team was quickly unhitched, watered, and turned out to graze and rest. They unloaded one of the water tanks, but left the other to be hauled to Jack's place later.

"We brought you something, Klara," Said Erik.

"Two somethings," said Ivar. He undid the canvas covering the back of the wagon. It wasn't the Sears princess model, but it was a well blackened cook stove with nickel chrome fittings.

"No wonder it took you so long. It must weigh a ton," said Torval.

"Not so much, but we walked the whole way to spare the team."

"How did you pay for it?"

"Ivar did it."

"He made drawings. At the railway station."

"While we waited to load the water tanks."

"Tell them, Ivar." Erik pushed Ivar towards Klara where he stood stuttering until his friends took over again. "Dead people. Two families were traveling east to bury loved ones. Ivar drew them in their coffins."

"So they would have something to remember."

"One of them was a child. Drowned."

"They paid good," said Ivar. "We bought the stove. And this." He handed Klara a light, bulky package.

"Muslin. We can cover the ceiling to keep the dirt from falling down."

"Enough for the window openings too. Until we get proper glass."

Klara hugged her brother. "I hope it wasn't too hard for you."

"Drawing dead people? I just pretend they sleep."

With the installation of the cook stove Klara became the official cook for the group. The stove provided a much easier means to cook the wild meat that Erik provided and light bread became a staple of their diet once Klara mastered the art of heating the oven and all the mixing and kneading. With the four of them keeping a watchful eye out Klara never lacked fuel for the hungry stove. The big drawback was that the heat generated to cook also made the small house unbearably hot.

That first year proved to be a good season for crops. The rain came at just the right time and the ten acres Ivar and Jack managed to subdue burst forth with a bumper crop of wheat and Milo. Torval built a smoke house to preserve the game they shot and soon had a trickle of customers asking to buy their cured meat. Other neighbors brought their own game to be smoked in trade for a portion. Klara found herself making more trips to the smoke house to serve customers than to her own flourishing garden. By fall the edges of all the fields held a bounty of winter squash and giant pumpkins. The hollyhocks grew so tall they obscured the front of the sod house.

The bounty of the season did not extend to the Lindblad homestead. Their new soddy was a small, windowless shack. The plow Arvid had neglected to return to a neighbor back on the Brule lay rusted in an unfinished furrow. The seed grain had been fed to the gaunt cow and Sophie had managed only a small garden. When her labor pains came, she sent Lily to find Klara. Arvid was away on a job.

"You actually live here?" said Klara.

Lily replied that it wasn't quite as nice as their home on the Brule, but she liked it well enough.

"Matty. Can you take the horses?"

"Mama's inside. It's cooler there."

Klara stooped to cross the threshold and nearly gagged at the stink of the place. She found Sophie huddled on the plank bed in the corner. "Where do the children sleep," she wondered aloud. "And eat." She noted that Sophie had more dishes, pots and pans than a half dozen families and all of them were crusted with filth and stacked in a wash tub on the table. A moan from Sophie made her forget the mess.

"Let's get a look at you, Sophie."

"I was afraid you wouldn't come."

"Won't be long now. This one is ready."

Klara stripped the dirty quilts from the bed and called for Lily to find something clean. And water. Before the hour was up the Lindblad family had another mouth to feed. Baby Emma had arrived.

With Lily's help Klara cleaned up the worst of the mess and fed the children. When she asked, Will showed her the old snake bite on his leg. It was still badly swollen, but seemed to be healing.

"Does it hurt?"

Will shook his head and tried to climb in bed with his mother.

Lily grabbed him by the shirt tail and pulled him away.

"You're not the baby any more."

Will limped to the corner where the yellow dog lay nursing a new litter. When the dog growled at him, he burst into tears and ran out into the yard to join his brother.

Not used to so many small dramas, Klara admonished Lily to

158

keep things clean and look after her mother. It felt like walking out from under a fierce black cloud when she left the Lindblad soddy. Her own place seemed like a palace by comparison. Torval met her in the yard and helped unsaddle the horse.

"I've a surprise for you," he said. "Come see."

In a dark corner of the partially finished barn Torval pointed to a burlap sack that was wiggling and flopping with a life of its own.

"What is it?"

"Take a look."

When Klara opened the mouth of the sack, a half dozen heads poked out. The half grown hens opened and closed their yellow beaks in greeting. They could barely contain themselves when she released them. A runty black rooster that had been stuffed under the hens hopped out and strutted around flapping his wings and puffing up his rumpled feathers.

Overjoyed, Klara hugged Torval and danced him around the room. "Thank you, thank you. I do love chickens."

"We have to be careful to shut them up at night," said Torval.

"The coyotes will get them otherwise."

"Maybe they'll set some eggs before cold weather."

"Then you'll have chickens to spare."

"I can sell them. And eggs, too."

~~~

Arvid had taken a job with the railroad, so Sophie saw him only a few days each month. When he was home he seemed like a different person. Loud, engrossed in repeating dirty jokes he had learned from his fellow railroaders, swigging from the flask of whiskey he carried everywhere, he frightened the children and had little to say except criticism. He was away working on the railroad when Will got snake bit and, again, when a month later, their fourth child, Emma, was born.

Then Arvid came home. For good, he said. He seemed to settle down. He hauled water and talked about getting a well digger. He played with baby Emma and taught Matty some new knife tricks. Best of all for Sophie they talked and flirted like in the old days. She even found one of her old dresses and put her hair up for him.

"There's gonna be a dance over at Meadow this weekend," said Arvid.

"Could we go?"

"I'll need some of that money. Can't show up in that wreck of a wagon."

Sophie gave up a major part of the homestead money and Arvid rode off towards town with a 'see you in a day or so.'

A few days later relief turned to frustration and anger when Arvid had not returned. When he did drag in, hung over and broke, he bragged about prospects of a new job. A rancher near Belle Fourche promised to pay him to guide visitors from back east as far as Deadwood. The dance and the new buggy were long forgotten.

Arvid had been home less than a week when a great cloud of dust appeared on the horizon. As the dust trail came closer, Sophie called the children to her.

"What is it, Mama?"

"Is it hoppers again?" said Lily.

"Or fire?"

Before long they could see that it was a large wagon of some kind. By the time the four horse hitch crossed the shallow gulley that marked their south boundary they could see that it was a handsome brougham coach. Even a layer of dust could not hide the polished mahogany body, the brass trim, the velvet side curtains.

"Get your father, Matty."

Arvid barely had time to slick back his hair and grab his hat before the carriage drew up at the front door. The horses trampled Sophie's poor struggling flowers and sent the chickens to roost in the sage brush. The lad at the reins apologized to Arvid, saying he tried to convince the women folk to wait in the hotel at Belle while he came for him. Arvid seemed confused, obviously furious with the driver, but wanting to be officious to the three women descending from the carriage. With a string of curses he sent the children into the house and tried to bully Sophie into retreating with them.

She stood numb and wooden, her mouth open with surprise and offense. With baby Emma at her breast she glared at the trio of women standing in her dooryard. When they stomped dust from their dainty patent leather shoes, Sophie became acutely aware of her own stringy hair and dirty overalls. She watched them remove their sweeping picture hats to better help each other pat and smooth already perfect hair-dos, shake out long flouncy dresses, and apply fresh lipstick to lips already crimson bright.

She pulled Arvid aside. "Why are they here? What sort of women are they."

He muttered something about them being entertainers and pulled away.

"Entertainers, my eye. That's a madam and her whores." Screamed Sophie.

"Calm down, Sophie. Please."

"Make them leave." A bubble of saliva seeped from her lips. Tears streaked her dusty cheek. "Now. Go away. Get out."

She clutched the baby hard to her breast. The poor thing set up a terrific howling, but Sophie paid no attention. She tried to drag Arvid away from the women.

"Predators! Vermin!"

Arvid shook off his wife's grip and pushed her aside.

He escorted the women back to the carriage, apologizing

about the lack of hospitality. Sophie ran after them screaming, but baby Emma slowed her too much. Arvid slammed the carriage door and jumped to the driver's seat to take the reins from the boy. Sophie pounded on the mahogany side panel, then thrust the baby at Arvid.

"Yours. Your spawn. How can you do this?"

She barely had time to jump aside when Arvid whipped the horses and turned the carriage around in the yard. Sophie looked like a mad women standing in the road throwing clods of dirt at them, screaming, barely keeping hold of baby Emma, her hair whipping, tears running black rivers down her face.

Dazed, Sophie staggered into the soddy and crawled into bed. When she had not moved by supper time, Lily took the baby from her. Matty, with little Will in tow, did his best to take care of the animals. They tried to feed the baby, but her screams discouraged them. Lily finally put the baby at her mother's breast and the screams subsided. The next morning, the bread and fat back gone, Matty bridled Arvid's saddle horse and headed for the Hanson soddy, some four or five miles away.

"Mama, Mama," said Lily. "Klara is going to come. Get up."

With Lily's help Sophie washed herself and combed her hair. Together they tended to baby Emma. It wasn't long before they could hear Torval, Klara, and Matty approaching.

"They'll think me a lazy slut," whispered Sophie.

"You need help, Mama."

"I can take care of us."

Sophie hurried around trying to set the house to rights, but the smell, alone, would send a body reeling.

Torval left immediately to haul water and fetch some cornmeal and bacon.

"What is it now, Sophie? Are you sick?" said Klara.

"I'm better now. You shouldn't have come."

"Where's Arvid? You shouldn't be alone."

"Off with his whores." Sophie's face mottled and she squeezed back tears.

With a burst of energy she hurled a bowl against the stove where it shattered into a dozen pieces. On her knees to pick up the bits she rocked back and forth.

"I'm so sorry. I shouldn't have yelled at him. I need to do better."

"It's not your fault.

"It is. I'm a terrible wife. I even hate the children sometimes."

"Nonsense. You need a good meal and a hot bath."

Sophie seemed to feel some better by the time Klara and Torval were ready to leave, but then she begged them to take baby Emma with them.

"Please, Klara. She'll be safe with you."

"Don't be silly, Sophie. Take care now."

Letters from Home

Mail had been sporadic because the weekly mail sack was dropped at the railhead, then entrusted to the first willing traveler heading south. The establishment of a post office at Meadow marked a new era on the prairie. A local man was hired to drive the mail between Lemon and Meadow. All but the bulkiest, heaviest items would be delivered. Civilization had come to Perkins County. Riding or walking to Meadow to check the mail became a part of life.

"Klara, we have a letter from Carrie," shouted Torval. "An answer to your card."

Appearing at the door drying her hands, Klara asked what Carrie had to say.

"She says she can't come now, but maybe in the spring."

"What about your parents?"

"She's not sure she should leave them just now, but everyone is reasonably well."

"No boy friend yet?"

"She doesn't mention one. She does say friends of hers, a married couple, are coming in September."

"It would be just like her to drop everything and come with them."

"They'll barely have time to build if they come this late."

"We can help."

"I hope they find land nearby."

"Isn't there an open section across the ridge from Jack's land?"

"I'll check and let them know about it."

~~~

A few weeks later a message arrived with the news that the Brynton party, including Miss Carrie Hanson, would await them at the rail station in Lemmon. Please bring a wagon to transport their household goods to their new homestead.

"Does it say where their homestead will be?" said Klara. "I hope it's close."

"No. I'd better tell Erik before he decides to take off with the big wagon."

Torval charged out the door leaving Klara to contemplate the niceties of having female companionship again.

A short time later Jack and Torval drove the big wagon into the yard. They were followed by Erik driving the light buggy.

"Come along, Klara."

"The work can wait," said Torval. "This will be a great holiday."

"Let me shut up the chickens." Said Klara. "Where's Ivar?"

"He volunteered to look after things here. In case we don't get back tonight. He'll feed the chickens."

~~~

The dusty travelers stood near their pile of baggage chatting with a tall fellow wearing sheepskin chaps and high boots. Jack halted the team. Klara climbed down and stretched her stiff muscles. When she caught sight of Carrie, she forgot the long bumpy ride and ran to embrace her.

"You have safe trip?" said Klara. "You look tired."

"This isn't much of a town is it?" said Mr. Brynton. "Livery, post office, saloon, dry goods, hardware."

"Wait till you see Meadow. This town actually has real buildings made from lumber. And a board walk out front."

"What's your plan?" said Torval. "Do you have land picked out?"

"Supplies? Horses?"

Mr. Brynton interrupted. "Mr. Pinto here says he has several relinquished claims for sale. Maybe we should look into it."

"Why use our money for land when we can have it free?" said Carrie.

"This relinquishment has a house and two acres ready to plant," said Mr. Pinto. "Save you a lot of labor."

He went on to extol the virtues of his particular piece of prairie until Torval asked its location. When he learned it was in Moreau Township, he turned away in disgust.

"That's way south of here. Really marginal land. Rocky and dry."

"There are several nice parcels adjoining our land," said Jack. "You'd be close to us and to Meadow."

Mr. Pinto replied that the railroad planned to run a line just south of the Moreau soon.

The members of the party argued the matter for some minutes. Mr. Brynton and his wife were firmly in favor of the established homestead on the Moreau. The two couples who had accompanied them were in favor of following his lead.

Carrie finally spoke her mind. "I'm staying here with Torval and Klara. I can homestead by myself just fine."

"Good girl," said Jack. "We'll help."

"Let's load your baggage," said Torval. "See what you need before we leave town."

In a bit of a huff the rest of the Brynton party left with Mr. Pinto to secure wagons and supplies. Torval and Jack looked over Carrie's baggage before Erik loaded it into the big wagon.

"You brought more stuff than all of us put together," said Torval. "Dishes, pots, quilts, salt, sugar, coffee. You're a wonder, girl."

"Look at this, Torv," yelled Jack when he pulled a canvas tarp from a pile of goods. "A scalding pot and skinning knives. Do you have a pig in here somewhere?"

Erik helped them heft the well blackened cast iron pot into the wagon.

"Gore, we can make soap and boil our dirty clothes too."

"It's the one we used on the farm," said Carrie. "I salvaged it when we moved to town."

"Glad you decided to throw in with us, Carrie," said Torval.

"You just love me for my scalding pot."

When the wagon was full, they piled the rest of Carrie's plunder in the buggy and headed for home. On the way out of town they passed the livery stable where the Bryntons were arguing with their guide over the merits of mules over horses.

"I hope they have a pocket full of greenbacks," said Jack. "That fellow will bleed them dry if they're not careful."

"Town folks," said Carrie. "All bluster and blabber."

~~~

The trip home was slow, but Carrie gave it the aura of celebration. At the halfway point they stopped to picnic on a hamper of surprises Carrie had brought from home. Tinned ham, mustard, and flat bread, apples and cheese provided flavors the homesteaders had not experienced in months.

"All this needs is a linen table cloth and a flagon of fine wine," said Erik. "We'd believe we were in Paris."

"I fear the illusion will fade when Carrie sees the sod houses."

"We'll stake her claim in the morning,"

"The view is nice over that way. See that you lay out her house to face east."

"And plan for some windows," said Klara. "We don't have nearly enough."

~~~

Work on the new homestead began the next morning. By week's end the claim had been filed and the walls of the tiny soddy stood shoulder high.

"If you weren't so blasted tall, Carrie, we could raise the roof supports now," said Torval who stood a head shorter than his sister.

"Don't get cheeky, brother," said Carrie. "Bring me another load of blocks."

Almost single-handedly, Carrie slung the heavy sods into place. Two more courses and the walls were declared finished. The roof followed. A sheet of precious tar paper was laid over the supports, then covered with more sod. With Klara's help they finished the interior walls and hung strips of flowered calico over the mud plaster. A small stove was placed against one wall and a corner cupboard installed.

"All done," said Torval. "You can move in."

"Not quite," said Carrie. From her stash of belongings she produced a piece of carpet that nearly covered the entire mud floor.

"What on earth," said Torval. "It looks familiar."

"From the old house. It was about worn out, but I cut a section that had been under the sideboard. Looks nice, doesn't it?"

"The only soddy in the county with an Oriental flare."

"Now I need paper lanterns and chop sticks."

"A door mat and a boardwalk would keep the house cleaner," said Klara.

"You girls work on that. Us men folk need to dig a privy," said Jack.

"Put it a long way off," said Carrie.

"You won't be saying that when the weather changes. It's a long hike through six foot snow drifts."

"At the Lawrence house we had indoor privy," said Klara. "So nice."

"It won't be happening here. We don't even have a well."

"It does rain sometime, doesn't it?" said Carrie. "I brought a rain barrel. We can put it out under the roof corner as soon as I unpack the dishes."

Jack and Erik carried the heavy barrel into the new house. Brand new with staves bright from a coat of varnish, it almost glowed in the morning light. When the lid was removed, the aroma of wood shavings filled the room.

"New wood. Why do you girls buy flowery perfume, when this new wood smell would attract fellows like flies to honey?"

"Idiot. Go dig the privy."

The fellows left Carrie and Klara to finish unpacking and setting the house to rights. They could hear them clucking to the team and joshing one another until they dropped below the hill behind the house. The privy would be out of sight at least.

"China? You brought China plates," said Klara. "And cups."

"Saucers, a gravy boat, dessert plates, serving platters, the works," said Carrie. "My mother's set. She gave it to me special."

"How many?"

"Service for twelve."

Klara counted on her fingers and gave up. "So many."

"We'll have a dinner party, a house warming."

Klara looked around the tiny house with its two chairs. "Twelve in here?"

Carrie giggled. "We don't have to use all the settings. And the fellows can build some benches."

They flopped down on the curve back settee to rest and survey the results of the day's work. Stuck on the subject of China cups and plates, Klara told Carrie about her mother's chocolate set.

"Handed down from her mother. A wedding present it was," said Klara. "I broke one of the little cups when I was five."

"Bet she tanned your hide good for that," said Carrie.

"She should have, but she just cried."

"A woman needs a few pretties in all this mess and bother."

They put the kettle on to boil for tea, rolled the barrel out into the yard, and cleaned up the wood shavings. The two women were sitting in the new room sipping oolong tea when the fellows returned.

"And don't you look a picture," said Torval. "Afternoon tea on the prairie."

Buy Low, Sell High: Profit on the Prairie

Soon other prairie wives were drawn to Carrie's comfy home. She had a stack of women's magazines and the kettle was always on. With Torval or Jack to help she set to breaking a few acres near the house. It was not too late to plant winter wheat. A small plot of lettuce and peas sprouted in the shade of the soddy watered by the wash water each evening.

When she saw dust on the horizon or heard hooves on the track leading to her home, Carrie would stop what she was doing and hustle to the house to stoke up the fire. Before long she had a ladies sewing circle organized. With bags of scraps begged from family back in Grand Valley the ladies were soon hard at work on quilts. Quilts for their own families and for the less fortunate.

After a particularly well attended sewing session she pulled Klara aside.

"These women hardly have a needle between them. And scissors. My goodness. We need supplies."

"The store in Meadow?"

"A joke. All seeds and axel grease and tools for the men."

"We could make an order from the catalog," said Klara.

"Yes. Then sell the things ourselves."

They spent the next few evenings studying the catalog, making a list, imploring Torval for help and advice.

"Ladies, ladies, if I knew how to retail goods, I wouldn't be breaking sod."

"But you worked in Uncle Jim's store," said Carrie. "You saw how it all worked."

"Pool your money, order your goods, and then we'll figure out how much you can charge."

170

Jack arrived on the scene and showed them a catalogue detail about ordering in bigger lots. "Ten needle packets at a time are cheaper than one at a time. Fifty are cheaper yet. Same for buttons and thread. And all these other sewing doodads."

"That's a big difference," said Carrie. "What about calico?"

"You'd have to buy a whole bolt to get a break there."

"We'd never agree on the color and pattern."

"That's easy. Just buy gray."

Both women burst out laughing at that comment. "Gray? Everything out here is gray, you dufus." Still chortling with laughter they hustled Jack out the door and sat down to finish their order.

Klara's experience with money had been limited, but she caught on quickly. She threw cold water on Carrie's notion that they could sell fifty needle packets and pay for most of their order.

"There are only eight in our group and some of them have plenty of needles."

"So we need to buy in lots of ten," said Carrie. "We won't make near as much."

"Button's. Can we mix up the colors and shapes?"

"Yes. Fifty button cards, then?"

Somewhat mollified, Carrie finished the order. They had thought long and hard about the calico and finally settled on a bright yellow with a small pattern of flowers. Every woman in Perkins County would be sporting flowered yellow calico come spring. With high hopes they mailed their order.

~~~

While Klara fretted over the slow arrival of their sewing supplies, Torval let slip the story of how he had acquired his mail order bike. Both Klara and Jack asked him why he had stopped riding.

"The front tire is shredded beyond repair," he answered. "Shot, kaput."

"Why don't you order a new one?" said Klara. "We didn't need to buy so many sewing things."

"Saving up for something else," said Torval. "Something that can handle this rough country."

"He wants an automobile, that's what he means to say," said Jack.

"Shut up, Jack."

"A horseless carriage? That's a joke isn't it."

"He saw one once and now he's got the bug," said Jack.

"Is it even possible?"

"Possible? It's the future," said Torval. "Hard roads and automobiles."

"Why don't you boys order a few extra supplies and start a dry goods store?" said Carrie. "Seed, tools, sugar, salt. You could earn enough money to finance your pipe dream."

"We could put up another soddy next to Carrie's. On that rise so we could see the customers coming," said Jack.

"Better yet. We build it east of Torval's house. Nearer the road." Said Ivar.

"Shall we do it?" said Carrie. "Build the store in our spare time and open in the spring."

"What can it hurt? If it all comes to naught, Torval will still have a new storage building."

"Or Klara can use it for a chicken house," said Carrie.

"Or a garage for Torval's auto," said Jack. "It will be fun."

"Strange boys. To think cutting sod fun," said Klara.

~ ~ ~

The Hanson bunch made short work of harvesting their ten acres of wheat and Milo. Klara and Carrie dug the potatoes and picked green beans and dry beans until their fingers ached. The squash, pumpkins, onions, and turnips were stowed in a hay-lined hole dug in the bank awaiting a proper root cellar. The fellows hired out to help with wheat harvest on neighboring claims. Prairie grass was cut and dried for hay and the gulleys and breaks scoured for firewood. Still they had time to raise the store building by working the twilight hours each day.

One of the more pressing jobs involved windows and doors for the soddys. The strips of muslin were quite adequate in the heat of summer, but little good in rain or snow.

At the first break in their work load Jack and Torval made a trip to Meadow in search of sawn lumber and windows. On their return they set to measuring and sawing the wood for the doors. An old timer passing by warned them to hang the doors to open inward.

"How come?" said Torval. "How can it matter?"

"Snow piles up against the door and you can't get out, that's why," he said.

"Surely not."

"Had to dig down through the roof to pull a family out. Over by Bixby last year. They were pert near suffocated by the time we got them out."

"No kidding?"

"You'll see. Mind you get it right."

Though they laughed and joked about the old man's admonition, they hung the new doors to open inward. It required some chopping of the doorways and some placating of the girls, but the doors on all the soddys opened correctly on their leather hinges.

"That door takes up space in the room," said Klara. "And brings in more dirt."

""Messes up my carpet," complained Carrie. "Surely it doesn't snow that much."

The windows proved more difficult. There was barely enough glass for one soddy.

"Sorry girls. We are going to cover up your fine windows."

"Divide the windows so we each get one," said Carrie.

"How about shutters," suggested Ivar. "Outside. Leave them open in good weather. Close them at night and when it rains."

"Or snows." Klara turned to Torval. "Please. It is so dark in here."

"Another trip to town, then. For more lumber."

"There's an abandoned house on Owl Cat Ridge." Ivar gathered up his tools. "Maybe we can salvage something."

"Good idea. We'll be back in time for supper."

~~~

The boys returned near midnight with the creaking wagon which they left in the yard to be unloaded in the morning. When the horses had been fed and watered, they clattered into the house to announce their success to the women.

"Short saw boards. Perfect for shutters," said Ivar. "Took some work, but we got them."

"The other scavengers either missed them or didn't want to take the time to pry them out," said Torval. "They were in an old shaft shoring up the dirt walls."

"Shaft? A mine?" said Carrie. "Wasn't that dangerous? What were you thinking?"

"Nice smooth lumber. Fairly clean too. It's been out of the weather."

"Got a sack of big spikes too. I'll pound them straight in nothing flat."

"Was there anything left of the house?" said Carrie.

"Not a plate or a dented pot. The walls looked like grassy mounds. We nearly drove by it."

Rage on the Range

~~~Sophia~~~

When Arvid finally came home, Sophie made a great effort to be cordial and welcoming. She was determined to be the good wife, but Arvid made her efforts difficult because he chattered endlessly about his last great adventure.

"Miss Bee thought I was so, so brave chasing away a thieving coyote." Arvid mimicked the high girlish tone of the absent Miss Bee.

"Which one was Miss Bee?"

"Miss Star hung on my every word."

"As if you ever had anything to say. Flattery for sure."

"Madame Smith encouraged me to share their private stock of French wine each evening around the campfire."

"You wouldn't know French wine from vinegar," said Sophie.

"Sophie, Sophie. It was just in fun." Arvid made a grab at her and got a handful of apron instead.

Sophie retreated into black silence and slammed plates on the table. Arvid ate his supper of bread and clabbered milk, but talked endlessly about the superiority of Russian caviar, beefsteak grilled to brown perfection, crisp lettuce and tomatoes tossed together with a sauce both sweet and vinegar tart.

"Salad. That's what they call it."

Sophie pushed her plate away and finished nursing baby Emmy. Arvid started another story, this one about Deadwood and the fine homes being built on the hill above the town. When she couldn't stand another word, she wrapped the baby in her worn thin, washed gray blanket and shoved her into Arvid's arms.

She made a futile attempt at wiping spit up from her shirt and ignored Arvid's attempt to hand baby Emma back. Where can I go to cry, she wondered.

Where could she go to cry her bitter tears. The house, a bare twelve by twelve room, had no private place; outside the board privy fumed the eyes and turned the stomach. Sophie fled across the yard to pour out her frustration in the cow shed.

Maybe Arvid would follow, she thought. Show me some concern: apologize and salve my wounded soul. Her hopes were dashed when she heard the splash of discarded wash water, followed by the crash of the bar across the door. She was locked out of her own house. She made a nest in the hay and cried herself to sleep.

If Arvid thought a night in exile would bring Sophie to her senses, he was mistaken. Cold and stiff, she resolved to find a way out of her own private hell on earth. She staggered back into the house and fixed breakfast. She fried bacon, mixed a batch of corn muffins, and opened a jar of wild berry jam. With the fresh milk and hot coffee it seemed a feast. The children ate the unexpected treats in silence trying to shrink into the shadows. Arvid barely noticed his food.

"About two miles up Old Hill Road, that's where I spotted her."

"Spotted who," said Sophie.

"A female coyote. Must have a den up in the rocks."

"What do you want with a varmity coyote?"

"Saw one in Deadwood. Tame. The fellow raised it from a pup."

Matty stopped eating to listen. "Can I come? I'd help."

"You bet," said Arvid. He gave Matty a punch in the shoulder. "We can probably make money with a tame coyote."

Bright-eyed and red-cheeked with excitement, Matty ran to get rope and a burlap sack.

"Get the shovel, too," said Arvid. "And gloves."

Matty was wheezing with the exertion by the time they loaded up and rode out of the yard.

Sophie thought to keep her son home, then decided the fresh air would probably be good for him.

It was dark when they returned on foot. Arvid led the way, carrying a coyote pup, trussed up and secured in a sack. Matty walked behind leading the horses. Neither horse would tolerate the smell of coyote. Both Arvid and Matty seemed exhausted, but they worked past midnight making a pen they thought would hold the animal.

When they dumped the pup out of the bag, it struggled so much they decided to leave it tied up until morning. At Matty's tearful insistence, Arvid untied its mouth so it could drink.

Death Comes in the Morning

~~~Klara and Sophia~~~

As summer moved into fall, Klara felt reasonably content. Except for the absence of trees, it was little different from her home in Sweden. Her garden had prospered and she had a huge crop of beans to string and dry. The beans would become dark and leathery as they hung in loops from the ceiling. Soaking and boiling with a generous piece of fat back or bacon made them edible again. The root cellar that replaced the hole in the bank held a good crop of potatoes, onions, and turnips. Ham and jerked beef from a neighbor's recent butchering filled the smoke house. They had eaten fresh pork all week and the men vowed they would have their own milk cow and a couple of pigs come spring.

She had quickly gotten used to the new door and the window shutters proved to be a great success. That they had cost nothing added to their charm. Ivar had painted patterns of prickly flowers and streaming leaves on all the doors and shutters. As a final touch he had added a 'welcome' sign to the doors. Both her soddy and Carrie's seemed snug and tight, impervious to winter's touch.

With a large needle and a strong thread Klara had whipped her way through most of a bushel of green beans when Lily rode into the yard. The speckled mustang she rode trembled with the effort and made no move to escape when the girl slid off. As disheveled as the horse, Lily pulled her skirt down and scrubbed her hair back from her face.

"Can you come? Please hurry."

"What is it Lily? Torval has the horse this morning."

"We can ride double. Please hurry."

"Let me find Torv. Your horse can barely walk."

"No. No, come now."

With Lily grabbing at her elbow Klara hurried to the post in the yard where a large bell hung. With a few strokes of the clapper she summoned anyone in earshot. When Torval rode into the yard expecting fire or pestilence, she explained the situation. He helped her mount his horse and gave Lily a leg up behind her. The pair rode off with the promise that he would follow with the mustang.

At the Lindblad place Klara found Sophie and Arvid in the yard with the children except for Matty. Matty lay still on the ground. For a boy was always into mischief, strong and quick like his father, it was odd indeed.

"Do something, Klara," sobbed Sophie. "Please, please."

"What happened?"

"He was fine last night. Fit as a fiddle," said Arvid.

"You," screamed Sophie. "You killed him."

"It's all that mollycoddling, woman."

"Maybe he's not dead," said Sophie. A glimmer of hope touched her voice.

"We need to examine him. Carry him into the house."

With Matty stretched out on the kitchen table Klara searched for a sign of life. Even her untrained fingers found no trace of pulse or breath. Matty was indeed gone.

The garbled story finally came out. The child was alive and racing to check on the coyote pup, the next moment he was stone still in the dooryard. No time to prepare, no time for good-byes.

"Me, why not me, God," wailed Sophie.

"You best be making arrangements, Arvid." Klara prepared to leave.

"Probably not even my kid," said Arvid. "Somebody's bastard."

"How can you say that?" Sophie's grief flashed to white hot anger. "He looks like you, walks like you, talks like you."

"You and all your men friends," said Arvid. "That's why."

"Years and years ago. Before we were married. And what about your whoring hussies."

Whatever bond that may have joined Sophie and Arvid tore and grew to a huge chasm that moment. Only Torval's arrival with the limping mustang silenced the combatants. Klara shook her head no to his silent question. They escaped the tense house and rode home.

~~~

Klara put the plight of her childhood friend out of her mind as she returned to her preparations for the coming winter. There was little she could do and there was much work at hand.

At the Lindblad soddy Arvid continued to blame Sophie, for everything. Scathing, scalding words flooded around her every time he thought of another man who might have fathered the dead Matty. When the tirade was over, she suffered a period of his silent, brooding punishment. Each time she would rack her brain to remember the details of her conduct with Arvid's accused and each time she found herself innocent of wrong doing.

As her despair grew, she found herself shredding her clothing or digging deep scratches into her own arms and wrists. At other times she would scream her anger silently and pound her fists into the mound of bread dough on the kneading board. Sometimes her tears dampened the leavened mass until she had to add more flour.

"How can you do this to me, Arvid? Dear God," moaned Sophie. "It hurts as if it happened yesterday."

"Shut up," said Arvid. "Get supper on, slut."

She looked down and realized she was gripping table edge so hard her knuckles were white. Her hands ached when she released her grip.

She relived that horrible scene over in her mind each time Arvid spoke. How she was jarred awake at first light by shouting in the yard. The surprise she felt when she found both Matty and Arvid already up and out.

By the time she had finished dressing she could hear Arvid swearing at Matty, calling him stupid and babyish. When she ran outside, she saw Arvid ducking under the low roofed shed with a handful of shredded rope in his hand.

Worst of all she watched Matty run across the yard towards the house. Over and over he ran across the yard. He never made it. Never. No matter how many times she replayed the scene. No matter how hard she willed him to her. He never made it across the yard. He always, always stopped half way and twisted a little, his mouth open. Then his eyes clouded over and he dropped like a stone to the hard packed earth. A tiny thread of blood marred his face.

Alone on the prairie Sophie let her screams echo against the sky. "Dear God, how could this happen? Why? Why?"

She threw herself to the rocky ground not knowing if she spoke aloud or screamed in silence. Not even in her worst nightmare had she seen herself kneeling in the dust holding her dead child, her firstborn son.

"Am I so horrible, God?"

Sophie pounded the earth with her bruised fists, pawed the dust like a wounded animal.

"Can my sin be so great that you deal with me like Pharaoh, back there in Egypt?"

When she finally got up and staggered back to the house, she barely remembered her tirade, her tears, or her agony.

Arvid hitched up the buggy and took poor Matty into town. The funeral was a few days later. Matty was buried in the cemetery at Bison, all alone. When the Lindblads returned home, they found the escaped coyote pup dead near the road. Perhaps it was too young to survive on its own. Sophie mourned anew as Arvid shoveled it into a shallow grave.

The Howling Winds of Doubt and Fear

Winter came late that year, but it came to stay. No Indian summer followed the first storm, nor did the icy blasts out of the north diminish in frequency. Carrie and Klara's parcel of sewing supplies arrived the day before the first storm and sat waiting on a shelf in Carrie's soddy. Food and fuel took precedence over such fripperies. Other mail, a letter and an awkward box, lay undelivered and waiting for the roads to clear. Klara would not have her news from home until after Christmas.

When the second storm roared out of the north, Torval and Klara awoke to a fine powder of snow on their feather tick. Snow coated the floor, table, and even the cold stove. Torval jumped out of bed and scrambled to find his clothes, socks and boots.

"Stay put, Klara." He tossed her things on the bed. "You can dress under the covers."

"How is the snow getting in here? We chinked it tight."

"Hard wind blowing. Must loosen the ceiling joists a bit."

He got the fire going, while Klara tried to sweep the snow into one corner. The room soon warmed and the kettle began to sing. Their thoughts turned to the horses and chickens in the lean-to barn. When Torval opened the door, a great cascade of snow rolled into the room. Snow to the roof line packed around the outside of the soddy.

"That old fellow was right," said Torval. "We'd have been stuck in here."

"I hope Carrie is all right. Do you remember if she had wood up?"

"Wish I had a shovel," complained Torval. He searched through Klara's household implements.

"We'll figure something after breakfast," said Klara. "Maybe the dustpan. Or the bread board."

After a hurried meal, Torval dredged and stomped a path to the barn where he found his shovel and fed the stock. At first light the wind died down and he was able to shovel a path to Carrie's soddy. Erik and Jack soon joined him to make short work of the snow removal. They found Carrie seated at her table with tea and cake set out for them. Ivar and Klara soon appeared with a great show of stomping their feet and shaking snow from their hats and scarves.

"Welcome to the party," said Carrie. "Our first snow party."

Though it snowed intermittently through the day, they ate and played cards with intermissions to tend the animals and stock the soddys with plenty of firewood. It was decided that Ivar would move in with Erik and Jack for the duration of the snow season. It would save fuel and lighten the work. There was some concern over leaving Carrie by herself, but no proper solution presented itself. Carrie insisted she was by far the most capable of the group anyway, so they decided to leave things the way they were for the time being.

The next storm dumped even more snow on the prairie. It stuck to every surface to produce a mirage of silver beauty. Ivar and Jack built a huge snowman and a snow fort, but Erik cut their frolics short when he announced the status of their dwindling fuel supply.

"We had so much wood up," said Jack. "Where did it go?"

"To keep your britches warm and cook your beans," said Erik.

"How the blazes do we scrounge wood in all this snow?"

"We don't. We make a trip to the XXX Mine and see if we can buy some coal."

Shallow seams of lignite coal could be found in the ravines near Meadow. The small mining company named XXX Mines operated at the biggest deposits, but a few enterprising fellows mined the black fuel in the smaller ravines. They sold it for a dollar a load.

With a great deal of groaning the boys dug the big wagon from its snow drift and went to inspect the harness. The cold leather was so stiff it could not be untangled without breaking so they lugged it into Klara's soddy to warm up. While the harness warmed, they led the team from the lean-to. Kept up without exercise for several days, the team plunged and kicked with wild excitement.

"Keep a good grip on those critters," shouted Torval. "You'll never see them again if you let go."

"Is it safe? What if it snows again?" said Klara. "Who is going?"

"Full of questions aren't you," said Torval. "Erik and Jack are going."

"We have the most experience," said Jack. "Big hunters find fuel."

"Big hunters, my eye," said Carrie. "Let me come along. I can drive the team and you two can shovel drifts."

"No way, Carrie. No ladies. We may have to sleep in the wagon, camp out."

"What can we do? Sit around and worry?"

"And keep the fire up and the chickens safe," said Erik.

"And have a big batch of biscuits and gravy waiting for us," said Jack.

"Venison stew and light bread, too."

"Better take a picnic basket with you," said Carrie. "I'll get it ready."

An hour later the wagon was still a dark smear on the horizon. It would be a long day, a long three days as it turned out

~~~

When the fellows returned, they found that Carrie, Ivar, and the chickens had moved into Klara's soddy. The need for warmth and water had won out over privacy and space.

"Mighty cozy in here," said Jack when he stooped to cross the threshold. "Gore. Warm, too."

"Did you get it," said Carrie and Klara together. They nearly knocked one another down in their rush to greet Jack and Erik. "Are you all right? We were so worried."

"Stiff and weary. Where's that grub you promised?"

Torval and Ivar grabbed their coats and ran to tend the tired horses standing harnessed to the low sagging wagon. They peered under the tarp.

"Looks like they got it."

"Hurrah for our side. Can we leave it on the wagon?"

"Don't see why not."

They led the tired horses into the stable and pitched them a generous mound of the dry prairie hay. A couple of handfuls of cracked corn and a vigorous rub down finished the job. They would bring them buckets of melted snow to drink later.

When they returned to the house, some of the black fuel was already giving new life to the cook stove where coffee simmered and eggs and sausage sputtered in the cast iron fry pan. Jack and Erik had a hat full of stories to recount between mouth fulls. Apparently this was only a tiny storm on the scale of all time blizzards. The two old timers minding the store at the XXX Mine had spun tales of gale force winds, ten foot drifts, and ice that encased the heads of men and beasts in giant ice balls.

"They said one family had to make bread from chaff and snow to survive."

"And another brought the three cows, a team, a dog, and four stranded visitors into their nine by nine shack."

"And worst of all was that they had to stay for three weeks before the storm let up," said Jack.

"Surly not," said Carrie. "Sounds like the good old days."

"We were lucky to get coal. They usually send it all to the rail head at Lemmon for the engines."

"Said they couldn't get drivers in this weather."

"Seems odd country for a coal mine."

"There are quite a few old shafts around here."

"Started by gold seekers when the big deposits were found at Deadwood."

"No such luck here. Just a little coal and some gluey gray stuff called bentonite."

"The fortune hunters all moved on in short order."

The coal haulers also brought home a new scheme. If they were to open a store, why not send an application for a post office to Washington. Torval was drafted to write the letter. Carrie would be the suggested post mistress.

The Gift and The Gifted

When the storm let up, the skies blued and the roads cleared. Both the wagon and the light buggy were rolled out, the team and Old Mack the buggy horse were fed, curried, and hitched up. The whole group piled in and headed for town with the yellow dog running between the wheels. The party air enfolded them all the way to Meadow.

At the post office Torval mailed his application to the proper government office and they took delivery of their month's mail. Letters from Canton, postcards from Carrie's old friends, two much handled letters from Sweden, and a box labeled 'fragile' complete with customs papers.

"From Pappa?" said Klara. She let Ivar read the return.

"No. It's Stina's hand writing," said Ivar. "I wonder what it could be."

"This ones from Winifred," said Carrie. "You remember her don't you Torv?"

"What's Winnie up to?"

Carrie adjusted her glasses and read, "*Was sure you had married and forgotten the rest of us by now.*"

"Are you? Going to marry and leave us," teased Torval.

Carrie sniffed and relegated the card to her handbag. "News from home, Klara?"

"Don't keep us in suspense," said Torval.

The first envelope held a stiff card of congratulations on their wedding. It bore scribbled signatures and a postmark months past. The second envelope was of thin, almost transparent paper. Klara held it at arm's length towards the light.

"It would be easier to read if you opened it."

"I can't. What if it is bad?" She handed the letter to Torval, who protested that he could only read Norwegian. Ivar took the letter and sat down on the boardwalk.

"In case it is bad news," he said. So Torval and Jack stowed the package in the buggy while Ivar tried to decipher the spidery handwriting. He was still stumbling over the scribbles and blots and odd phrasing of Stina's letter when Erik returned to inform him of their decision to do some shopping before returning home. Ivar folded the letter and placed it in his wallet.

"I think everyone is okay," he reassured Klara. "I'll work on it more when we get home. Stina is trying to write English and it's a bit of a muddle."

"I miss her," said Klara.

"She's a good sister."

At the general store the group took special note of the goods offered and questioned the storekeeper about sales and profits. They were much encouraged when the store owner offered to sell them a portion of his bulk orders at almost wholesale prices. The isolation of the Hanson and Hanson Dry Goods and Grocery would prevent it from being a competition to his own store.

"You should put up a false front. And a flag pole, maybe. Let folks see where you are from as far away as possible. These advertising cards are good too." He showed them postcards with pictures of himself standing in front of his establishment. "You can mail them too."

"Best get the store built first," said Carrie. "We need lamp oil. Flour and a wedge of cheese."

"A few pretties too," said Klara. "After all it's the holidays." She picked out a tinsel garland and a length of red ribbon.

"Matches and a whetstone," added Torval. "A nickels worth of horehound and a pound of nails."

The storekeeper advised buying several rolls of light rope. To guide the way between house and barn when the blowing snow obscured landmarks. He had a dozen tales of homesteaders frozen to death a few feet from their own front doors.

Several sacks of oats, cracked corn for the chickens, and a half load of rough sawn lumber completed their shopping.

By the time they headed home the skies were dark and

threatening. Erik led with the slower wagon. The team trotted out willingly now that they were headed for home. The wind was howling new snow out of the north by the time they reached home.

Tracks and scuff marks in the new snow brought out exclamations of surprise and question.

"A visitor?"

"Who'd be out in this weather? Someone on the lam. Thieves maybe."

"Maybe he's just lost," said Klara.

"He must be in the lean-to. No tracks to the house," said Torval. "Go inside ladies. We'll check this out."

A few minutes later a scruffy fellow with Torv and Erik at his elbow burst into the house. He had a long beard, light blue eyes, and a ragged pack. Pale soft fingered hands protruded from his too short sleeves. When he saw the ladies, he whipped off his battered hat and bowed. A fit of coughing cut short his greeting.

"He was burrowed into the hay with his donkey stretched out beside him."

"Says he's an artist. From Switzerland or some such place."

"J. L. Besler at your service ladies," said the intruder. "Call me Bez."

"Probably harmless, but Erik will stand guard while we tend the horses."

The stranger sat down and watched Klara and Carrie build up the fire and light the coal oil lamps. Coffee simmered on the stove by the time everyone gathered in the soddy. Carrie commanded the stranger to help himself to bread and jam. A plate of cold sausage was passed around the table. Unable to restrain himself, Bez forked two of the fat morsels onto his bread and downed the sandwich in three bites.

"Gore," said Torval. "When did you eat last?"

Carrie passed him more food and the whole group sat gawking at the stranger. He was far younger than first impression. Removing his hat and coat had revealed a head of thick hair spilling over thin shoulders. His whole body convulsed at his periodic coughing spells.

"It's my lungs," he explained between bites. "The doctors recommended I go west. For the air they said."

"Consumption most likely."

"You'll be dead of cold and hunger first. Sleeping in barns and such in this weather."

"Well, Thanks for the food. I'll be on my way now."

"Nonsense," said Carrie and Klara in unison. "We have room."

"And there's a new storm coming."

"He can bunk with us," said Erik. "Leave that idiot donkey here though."

Weary from the day's adventure, they agreed to worry through Stina's letter and open the package the next morning.

~~~

When the breakfast things were cleared away, Klara placed the package on the table. Her hands shook a bit as she cut the dirty string. Bits of excelsior spilled out to revel knobby paper-wrapped objects. With great care she unwound the layers that protected the tiny cups of the chocolate set. The tall, footed pitcher she saved for last. It emerged unharmed from its many layers of paper.

"Whatever possessed you, Mamma," whispered Klara. "How could you?"

"It's beautiful," said Carrie. "Where can we put it? It needs a fine walnut cabinet. Or at least a shelf of its own."

"From one poor house to another," said Ivar.

"Do you have any idea why Mamma would do this?" said Klara. "Did she not speak ill of me? She never wanted me to leave."

"She never spoke of you, Klara. Not once."

"Maybe the letter holds the answer."

"Ah, the letter. If we can decipher it."

Carrie found a pencil and tore out a page size sheet of the wrapping paper. Seated at the table she commanded Ivar to read the letter. As he puzzled through the lines one by one, Carrie wrote it down. Klara brought out her Swedish-English dictionary to help with the work. Finally Ivar and Carrie declared the job finished.

"It is the best we can do," said Ivar. "Now we read it through."

"Dear Klara and husband,

I hope you are well, Sister. Sad for me to hear you are married. Now I know you not return to us. I miss you. So does Mamma. With us not so good. Pappa is not yet working after mine accident. The boys are healthy. They run wild and don't do their chores sometime. Too many girls to chase after. Is Ivar working hard and not much trouble? I wish I could send a picture of baby Naomi all grown up. Mamma is not good. I afraid for her. And us sometimes.

Your loving sister
Stina"

Ivar agreed to draft an answer and left Klara to figure out what to do with the old porcelain chocolate set. After dithering a bit she asked Carrie if she could leave it at her place. It should be safe with her pretty things she reasoned.

"And you wouldn't have to feel guilty every time you see it," answered Carrie. "I know."

~~~

The over-night stay of the wandering artist stretched into weeks. Though Bez slept in Erik and Jack's soddy, he set up his easel at Carrie's place. The small house soon reeked of oil paint and turpentine. While everyone else worked at winter chores, he sat hunched over his brushes. The yellow dog joined in when Bez asked permission to use him as a model. The girls thought the rest would be good for the traveling painter, but Torv and Erik insisted he needed more exercise than that provided by his daily trudge between the soddys. Jack opined that it was the paint fumes that were killing their visitor.

Ivar was both fascinated and repelled by the itinerant artist. The man had a pack crammed full of the most wonderful array of paints and brushes which he shared freely. But just when Ivar thought he had the fellow figured out, he would find him pouring over a single brush stroke.

"You wipe that out again?" said Ivar. "Ten times now."

"Not right. Not right."

"It looks fine to me. What is it?"

"Light. I paint the light."

"In this dim place? I think you paint the dog."

"Dog is light. You are light." Between coughing fits Bez danced his brush across the canvas in a series of twisting strokes. "I see this in Paris."

"Maybe you should go back to Paris," said Ivar. "I don't even see the dog."

"There, you peasant," roared Bez. He hurled the canvas across the room and doubled over in a fit of coughing.

But, despite his dark moods, Bez finished the painting. Even Ivar was forced to admit it captured the yellow dog's mercurial soul perfectly. The next day Bez presented the picture to Klara with a bow. He kissed her hand and thanked her for the hospitality.

"Now I must be on my way."

"But you are sick," said Klara. She placed the still wet painting on the table."

"All the more reason. I need to get to California. My brother is there."

"It's only February," said Torval. "More storms will come."

"It looks clear now. I'll head south towards Deadwood. I have a friend there."

"That's a long way," said Torval. "We know people on the Moreau. They can put you up at least one night." He scribbled a map and wrote a short note to the Bryntons. Bez placed it in his sketch book, mounted the reluctant donkey, and rode off.

After the dog painting dried, Klara pounded a spike into the kitchen wall to hold it. Ivar fingered the tube of cobalt blue and the sable brush that Bez had left on his bunk. Both were amazed at the impact one skinny coughing man could have on their memories.

~~~

Throughout the year the Hansons inquired of the neighbors, the mailman, and various traveling salesmen, but none had news of Mr. Besler and his donkey. Perhaps he made it to California, perhaps he was the owner of the skull that washed down Owl Creek in the spring rains two years later. Ivar and Jack hiked up the gulley that contained Owl Creek when the spring floods subsided. They searched diligently, but found nothing.

One Step Forward, Two Steps Back

Between snow storms work on the store progressed. While the ground remained frozen, sod cutting halted. Plans for a frame structure were substituted and more used lumber was scrounged from several newly abandoned claims. Sheets of tar paper extended their materials and finally enclosed the four sides of the flimsy building.

"A stiff wind will send these walls sailing across the prairie," said Torval.

Jack advocated anchoring the building with ropes. "We can at least retrieve the pieces without chasing them plumb to Meadow."

When they were finished, the strangely tall building could be seen for miles. It seemed to waver in the harsh winter sun. Several neighbors stopped by to add their comments to the mix. Most felt the store a good idea, but worried that the false front which provided such a drawing card would also be its downfall. Customers were lining up before Jack and Torval finished stocking the shelves. By evening they had sold everything and sat in front of the stove in Torval's soddy making a list for the new inventory.

"You know," said Jack. "We could get this stuff cheaper in Bison."

"That's an overnight trip. Risky in this weather," said Torval. "But a night in town sounds like fun."

"We want to come too," said Carrie. "We can stay at the hotel, have a nice dinner. It's been ages since I had a night out."

"Gore," said Jack. "There won't be room for many supplies."

"A blizzard might leave us stuck someplace eating melted snow."

"We need to make an order from the catalogue," said Klara. "With today's profit we can get material, ribbon, thread."

"Why not wait for spring? We'll plan a real holiday."

"Send your order with us and we'll make a quick trip of it. Sleep in the wagon and be home by dark the next day," said Erik.

Reluctantly Carrie and Klara agreed stay home.

"You too, Ivar. You'll be more help here."

~~~

Late the next night a monster storm roared into the Dakotas from the north. There was little the three could do except keep up the fire and worry. Ivar tied one of the ropes around his waist and struggled through the blinding snow to bring the chickens into the kitchen. Even the short trip to the lean-to for coal proved tediously slow. A bucket full at a time, Ivar lugged it into the house. When the pile sat higher than the table, he decided it would have to do. There was little else they could do except worry.

By the third day they were sleeping in shifts to keep the fire up. The coal pile had been replenished several times. The chickens were reduced to eating dry bread and potato peelings. Between naps and keeping the fire up they played endless rounds of cards. When they could no longer stand to play one more variation of hearts or ten, Ivar painted vines and flowers on the cupboard fronts and the girls did needle work. The light was too dim and fingers too stiff from cold to manage very much fine work and they would soon be back playing cards. No one dared mention the missing travelers. They could only hope they were holed up in Bison enjoying town life.

Late in the afternoon of the third day, the snow stopped. For a half hour or so everything was still. The sun burned through the clouds low on the horizon and turned the dim landscape to a blaze of crystal. Ivar and the girls dug themselves out of the soddy once again and stood atop a drift surveying the countryside.

"This snow crust is hard as rock," said Carrie. She stomped it with her foot.

"Deep too. You can barely see the chimney."

"Hardly any snow around the store though." Ivar pointed north. "Must be the wind pattern."

"Can you see anyone on the horizon?" said Klara.

"No way they will be out there," said Ivar. "Maybe tomorrow."

Just before the light wavered to evening darkness, the wind

picked up. By the time the trio reached the doorway it exploded gale force. The store front buckled and kicked its way free of the rest of the building. It sailed past the soddy trailing broken boards and littering the snow crust. The walls followed with a murderous rain of debris. Mesmerized, Klara stood watching the work of many days hurl across the prairie. In the last light of the setting sun Ivar pushed Klara and Carrie through the soddy door and crashed it shut. A few trailing boards banged against the soddy roof before the howling wind blotted out the world.

~~~

Much of the snow had melted before Erik, Jack, and Torval plodded home. The news they brought over-shadowed the destruction of the store.

"Our neighbors, your friend, Sophie. You won't believe this," said Jack.

"She's in the hoosegow," said Erik. "Murdered her skunk of a husband."

"What? Surely not."

"Dead as a door nail is what I heard."

"They found her wandering around in her undies just before that last storm."

"Covered in blood we heard. Crazy as a loon. Babbling and screaming."

"The children? Oh poor Lily. And the baby," said Klara.

"She didn't hurt them. They're with a family in Bison."

Slow Grieving, Swift Justice

~~~*Sophia*~~~

How easy it was to pick up that ax, thought Sophie. She could glimpse it sitting there on the evidence table, she still felt the slight curve of its handle, the balanced weight of its steel head. A single bit ax, one edge honed sharp, the other a worn hammer head, one of the tools they bought just before they left Montana for the homestead.

Sophie shivered and pulled her shawl closer around her shoulders. Most of the observers in the court room wore their coats and the jurors had the benefit of the wood heater on the far side of the courtroom. The judge had his robe and the lawyers were never still long enough to feel the March chill. Only the poor woman transcribing the proceedings seemed as cold as the defendant.

How can she sit there day after day writing down the horrible things being said, wondered Sophie. Her expression never changes, even when she records the depth and location of the twelve ax wounds they found on Arvid's head and body.

The monolog in Sophie's head repeated over and over unrelenting. How unreal it felt to be reliving those painful hours of the past while she sat in the bleak courtroom. One would have thought her attention would be riveted to each word spoken against her, each motion, each maneuver by the earnest young lawyer hired in her defense, yet she heard nothing of the morning's proceedings.

All she could think of was that terrible morning. It filled her mind and flooded through her whole body. It even blotted out Mattie's death and that bleak plot of new broke ground in Bison Cemetery. It over rode all thought of her own uncertain future held in the hands of these strangers.

Arvid and I started ranting at each other. What had he been thinking, dragging that child along on his coyote hunt, keeping him up all hours, getting him over excited. Couldn't he see that Matty was flushed, exhausted. Arvid tried to distance himself by denying Matty was his son, accusing me of unspeakable things. Attacked, my resolve crumbled. I turned the blame on myself. Why had I let Matty go with Arvid, why didn't I speak up when I saw his flushed face, his rapid breathing. Why didn't I take better care of him. Hold him, keep him from harm.

When Arvid found he had the advantage, when he saw me turn the blame inward, he became aggressive. He stalked around the small room, a room made hot, oppressive by too much fire in the stove. He seemed to grow until he filled the whole house with his anger. When he reached out and grabbed me by the shirt front, I thought the Devil, himself, grappled me. I tried to shove him away, but he held tight and slapped me hard enough to snap my head back.

Stop screaming, stop.

I heard the words, but didn't know whose mouth screamed, who demanded silence. Arvid hit me again, with his fist this time. I slumped against him and he pushed me against the hot stove. Frantic to escape, strong with pain, I reached for a length of stove wood. My hand closed on the smooth, familiar ax handle instead. With the long ingrained motion of chopping wood, I arched my back and raised the ax over my head. The blade hit the low ceiling and bounded forward to strike Arvid over the left ear. It was a glancing blow, but it dazed him. When he staggered out into the yard, I followed. He tripped and fell against the pen he had built for the coyote pup. I could stand it no more. I raised the ax again and again. Would his screams ever stop, I wondered, then I realized it was my voice. It rose to meet the screams of the children huddled in the doorway.

The scene played through Sophie's mind, over and over. How can I ever forget it, thought Sophie. I stand frozen. I still hold the ax. Why doesn't Matty take the children and the baby somewhere safe. Hours later the neighbors found me wandering in the sagebrush, holding the ax tight to my breast. When I asked about the children, they assured me they were fine. Fine? How can anything ever be fine again.

In the tiny cell of the new county jail Sophia sat twisting her skirt edge to a rag. She ranted and babbled to anyone, or no one, within earshot. "Fine? How could I be fine if Matty is dead?" Her voice rose to a scream. "Did I kill him? Did I?"

A passing janitor paused to look at her. He shook his head and went about his job of mopping vomit from the cell next door.

"Who are you to pass judgment on me," she shrieked. "No more judging here."

The man looked at her and shook his head again.

"What more can I take. Arvid and Matty are dead. I finally understand that. Lily, Will, and baby Emma have gone to live with strangers. They'll no doubt end up in the orphan asylum. The livestock auction was months ago. Without heat and upkeep, the sod house will crumble into the dirt, the plowed fields will grow up in thistles, wind and rust will carry off the last of our few possessions. It will be as if we never lived. Can you pass a judgment worse than that? Can you? Can You?"

The next time Klara and Torval drove by the Bison Court House they saw a pile of green lumber stacked near the building. Carpenters were at work on a new gallows out back. The first woman, and the last, to be hanged in the Dakotas waited in her cell.

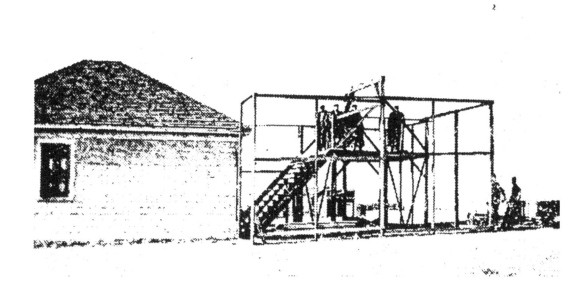

The Gallows Behind the Court House

Prairie Lilies And
The Pursuit of Happiness

Spring swept into Perkins County early. Goldenpea, bluebells, gilia, and phlox, followed by gumbo lily and a host of dandelion. The blooms painted the dingy landscape bright. Klara nearly wept when she found a clump of fritillaria in a shady gulley near the house. The little bell-shaped blossoms so reminded her of the flowers of her old home in Sweden she could barely speak. Torval found her sitting by the patch of funny looking speckled flowers.

"Klara, are you okay? I was worried."

She looked up and burst into tears.

"Hey, hey. It can't be that bad." He stooped to give her a hand up.

"Don't mash the flowers," she yelped. "Please, Torv."

"What's wrong, Klara?"

"They're so pretty. We need to make a fence. Keep the critters away."

"You frightened me. Running out like that. Come finish breakfast."

"I'm sorry you worried. I felt sick, then I found the flowers."

Torval took a long hard look at his wife, then hooked his arm in hers and steered her out of the gulley. "Let's go see Carrie."

Carrie, back in her own soddy after the winter storms, saw them coming and put the kettle on to boil. A nice cup of tea solved most problems, she thought.

"She was sick at breakfast," said Torval.

Klara interrupted, "I keep crying for no reason."

Carrie gave Klara a hug. "You're probably going to have a baby."

Klara turned pale and burst into tears again.

"Hot diggity," said Torval.

"Have to grow up little brother. You won't be the baby any more."

When the kettle whistled, she reached Klara's ancient chocolate pot from its shelf, added tea and hot water. She polished three of the pretty cups on her apron and placed them on the table.

"A proper celebration, that's what this is," she said.

Made in the USA
Columbia, SC
17 September 2018